BRAVE GIR

MW01068812

JETT JAMISON
& the Secret Storm

KIMBERLY BEHRE KENNA

Black Rose Writing | Texas

The author grants the final approval for this literary material.

First printing

This is a work of fiction. Names, characters, businesses, places, events, and incidents are either the products of the author's imagination or used in a fictitious manner. Any resemblance to actual persons, living or dead, or actual events is purely coincidental.

ISBN: 978-1-68513-243-9
PUBLISHED BY BLACK ROSE WRITING
www.blackrosewriting.com

Printed in the United States of America
Suggested Retail Price (SRP) $19.95

Cover art by Steph Mullins stephsayshello.com

Jett Jamison and the Secret Storm is printed in Calluna

*As a planet-friendly publisher, Black Rose Writing does its best to eliminate unnecessary waste to reduce paper usage and energy costs, while never compromising the reading experience. As a result, the final word count vs. page count may not meet common expectations.

For Elizabeth

Praise for
JETT JAMISON
& the Secret Storm

"Readers will love the memorable and realistic cast of characters in this tale of a sixth-grader's journey to discover the mystery of a suppressed library book. Along the way, she will discover answers to the difficult storm brewing inside herself, as well as find her voice to advocate for both. Jett is a brave, compelling character, and this novel is an engaging and inspiring take on a sensitive topic. An important read!"
–Sonja K Solter, award-winning author of *When You Know What I Know*

"Jett Jamison has a secret—a deeply painful one. She also has determination, a strong sense of justice, and a wide open heart that will have young readers glued to her side and rooting for her as she works to stop a censorship campaign against a book she knows she needs to read in order to heal. With bravery, beautiful writing, and just the right amount of restraint, Kimberly Behre Kenna has opened the door for a crucial and overdue conversation about sexual abuse and survival for middle grade readers. More than twenty years ago, teenagers were given the gift of Laurie Halse Anderson's *Speak*. Now, finally, pre-teens have this stunning and necessary book."
–Ona Gritz, author of *August or Forever*

"In *Jett Jamison & the Secret Storm* Kenna has done that rare and wonderful magic trick of immersing the reader into the psyche of a tender tween soul in crisis without any dissembling or subterfuge. The story *breathes* with subtle and deft nuances of insight and feeling—the microcosm of a garden is given equal definition to the larger issues of unacknowledged abuse and the way we as a community rebuild from these crimes together. The reader of any age enters into Jett's world of pitfalls and trauma from the first page, though they quickly learn that Jett is no frozen victim: she's a fighter, a detective, and when it counts the most, a trailblazer. The town of Wisteria can be found in Anywhere, America that hasn't learned from the *Scarlet Letter*, that tries to separate the Other from its forever home inside Us. This unassuming but also unabashed book will do wonders for the heart and spirit of young people grappling with silence where an open conversation could change their lives forever."

–JR Potter, award-winning teen mystery author of *Thomas Creeper and the Gloomsbury Secret*

"Sixth-grader Jett Jamison relies on carefully curated lists and schedules to protect her from the stress of a chaotic family life and the jumbled fragments of a disturbing memory. But an unexpected friendship and a mysterious book challenge Jett's beliefs about the value of predictability and order and embolden her to face those who have silenced her and others. Kimberly Behre Kenna tackles a difficult subject with the perfect balance of honesty and hope in her portrayal of a courageous and relatable heroine whose observations about herself and the world sparkle."

–Linda B. Davis, MSW, author of *Food Fight*

"Even in the mud and scum of things,
something always, always sings."
–Ralph Waldo Emerson

JETT JAMISON
& the Secret Storm

CHAPTER ONE

I stand on tiptoe and reach way up past the everyday graffiti, past the proclamations about who loves who and cartoon sketches of the most unpopular teachers. My tee-shirt scootches up, and I gasp when my bare belly touches the icy wall. I tuck the shirt into my jeans and reach up again.

Dad calls it a criminal act. I argue that if done respectfully, it's more like speaking out. I looked it up. The definition of vandalism includes the word *malicious*. I am not malicious. I do what I do to remind myself of where I've been and where I'm going.

The piney smell of disinfectant stings my nose, so I breathe fast through my mouth as I carve a straight line into the stall's wall, parallel to the other seven tally marks, each a thumbnail apart. Metallic flecks speckle my hand like glittery snow. My breath slows. The sharp scrapes of metal on metal promise that my marks will last longer than the fading ink of the words and pictures below them.

I am stronger than they are. I am.

I tweak the new tally just a bit, ever so carefully so all the lines stand nice and even like rails on a fence.

Perfect. Task complete. I settle down onto the toilet seat. A stream of sunlight spills from a high rectangular window onto my arm, flickering the metal in my hand. I press the sharp point with my thumb. With just a bit of force, I could draw blood with my trusty can opener. A powerful tool makes for a powerful person.

But hiding out in a foul-smelling restroom eight times in less than a month doesn't exactly make me a daring, brave wonderkid. My tallies tell it all. This is becoming a bad habit. I am not getting better, and I'm definitely not getting braver.

The outside door shushes open and thunks closed. "Jett! Are you okay?"

I settle further down into the seat and hold my aching head in my hands. "Yes. I'm fine, Thellie. Go back and finish your lunch."

"Come with me. My mom packed cookies."

My stomach pitches. "I'll be there soon. Just finishing up."

"Is it because of what Gina said?"

"I could care less about Gina."

"Right. Doesn't matter what Gina says. Our graphic novel could be on the road to bestseller for all she knows. You free after school today to finish up Part Two?"

"Not sure, Thellie. I don't think so. Can I just get some privacy in here?"

"Okay, but come out soon because Mrs. Langley's asking about you."

The door closes. Mrs. Langley is one of the cafeteria ladies. She's nice but nosy.

I slip the can opener into my backpack and run my hand over the new tally on the wall. The rough indentation feels good. To the left are last month's tallies. Only five in April. The month before that, three. Some studies say it takes one hundred twenty days to break a habit. That gives me about five more weeks. Then, all bets are off on me and bravery. I've got to quit running away to this restroom. But, oh how the silence in here calms my heart right back to where it belongs.

The door opens again, and a bunch of sneakered feet tramp into the restroom.

"Oh, Je-ett, where are you?" someone singsongs snidely.

"No use hiding. I can see your sensible tie shoes under the door." The girls giggle.

"Did things get a bit too noisy for you at lunch?"

Ding-ding-ding!

Thank goodness. The bell.

"Talia, let me borrow your lip gloss before we go to class. Hurry or we'll be late."

"Bye-bye, Jett. Oops, maybe I should've whispered." Gina clears her throat. "Bye-bye, Jett," she whispers. "I hope everything comes out okay." They leave the restroom chattering like crows.

I stand and look down at my feet. My shoes might be sensible, but my mind makes no sense at all. Loud noises make me race for cover like a soldier on a battlefield. And the cafeteria isn't even the worst of it. The non-stop voices in my head are. And they hurt. Bad. But it's better that kids think I'm hiding from noise. That seems less crazy than hiding from voices only I can hear.

·   ·   ·

After school, the day doesn't improve any at home. Mom's at the kitchen sink rinsing blueberries for a pie, and Dad's working on his sketches at the table.

I toss a bag of glass shards into the trash. Mom looks up. "What was that?"

"My life. A broken mess."

Mom retrieves the bag and carefully opens it.

"Bo and Jack, Mom. They invaded my bedroom, started wrestling, and broke my favorite snow globe. It nearly ruined my Hatshepsut book. I'm lucky they didn't kill poor Felix while they were at it."

"Felix will be fine. He's in a cage." She puts the bag in the garbage and goes back to rinsing.

"He's a helpless bunny! I'm in charge of his safety!"

"Calm down, Jett. You can't expect third grade boys to be quiet all the time." Mom dabs the blueberries dry with a towel. "And that sign on your door is a bit much, don't you think?"

"Why? It's a do not disturb sign. It clearly states that every two hours on the hour, I'll open my door for five minutes of consultation if needed. Seems pretty reasonable to me."

"Sometimes they just want to play with their big sister," Dad says.

"I've got a shoebox full of one hundred thirty-three To-Do Lists. No time for play."

Schedules and plans make my parents crazy. Not having schedules and not planning make me crazy. I pluck a blueberry from the towel and slowly squish it between my fingers till it's mush.

"How can anybody be calm in a house where kids think they're super-heroes? For once, can't you just be on my side?" My parents believe kids should run free and be themselves. But I've never been able to finish even one chapter of a good book in my noisy House of Horrors. Not in any one of the six we've lived in so far. "Seriously, I'm better off living at the library. Maybe I'll come home to sleep. Okay?"

Mom eyes the smashed berry and points at the sink. "Clean up. And go ahead to the library."

"Thank you, Mom, a thousand thank-yous!"

"But do come home to sleep," she adds with a smile.

I don't find any of this one bit funny.

In every town we've lived, the library has been my hideout. Quiet. Everything in order. No surprises. We've been in the town of Wisteria for nine months, moved here from Stonewall where we lived next door to my aunt and cousins. My parents say house-hopping is "a healthy opportunity for kids to experience diverse people and places." But I'm too old to be fooled. My mother and aunt had a huge fight, and in the Jamison family kingdom, fights are forbidden. Loyalty is law.

We moved in with my Mimi. My mom's mom. Good thing because she needed extra help when she got sick. Mimi was the only one who understood me. She said we were on the same wavelength, the wavelength of peace. I need to keep the peace in her honor. It's the least I can do.

But now, without Mimi around, noise oozes from every corner, drips down every wall, and slips under closed doors like smoke. Just like all the other houses we've lived in.

Back in my bedroom, I jam my books into my backpack and then pull one of my little wooden dolls off the bookshelf. I cup her in my hands like an egg in a nest.

"Mimi?" I say to her, "The voices in my head are back. Give me a sign. Tell me what to do."

My Mimi collected nesting dolls called matryoshkas, and every birthday since I turned nine, she gave me one. This pink one is my favorite doll, the first Mimi gave me. Each of my three dolls is slightly different, brightly painted girls holding flowers, and when you twist the top off, inside is another doll that also twists open to reveal another, and another, until there are six complete dolls, each one smaller than the one before it. One doll, not much bigger than my palm, carries five more inside her like hidden treasures. Whenever I need help, I talk to my dolls, sure that bits of wisdom nest inside them, same as my wise grandmother.

I trace the doll's dress with my finger. "Mimi, I'm doing everything in my power to find peace, but it's not meant to be."

I hold the doll closer. Each of her tiny white teeth is distinct except for one with chipped paint that gives her a lopsided smile. I like the imperfection because it reminds me of the gap in my own front teeth. When I place my tongue behind them just right, I can make a shrill whistling sound like a steam kettle at boiling. A bit like a screech. I hardly need to part my lips to release the sound.

Jett Jamison. Ventriloquist.

Mimi told me I should pucker up my lips and do a full-on whistle—mega-loud—to let the entire universe know where it's coming from. I'm not quite ready to do that. I like being anonymous. It's safer.

CHAPTER TWO

Walking toward the town green, the heat from the asphalt sears the bottoms of my rubber flip-flops and seeps into the soles of my feet. I pick up my pace, shifting my backpack so the skin under my damp tee-shirt can breathe. Summer's coming. Sixth-grade graduation is a little over a month away, but our next move is creeping closer. Dad's an architectural consultant and Mom's a seamstress, so it doesn't matter where they live. They can find customers anywhere and work from home. I'm not about to get too attached to a town or a house or friends knowing we'll be gone in a year. Up and vanished, like chalk on a sidewalk.

People love this town. Wisteria is named for the lavender-blue plant that pops up all over the place. It clings to fences, winds around lamp posts, creeps up sides of houses. Its blossoms smell sweet like sheets fresh from the laundry.

Beautiful, right?

Not quite.

Wisteria grows so fast it takes over gardens if you're not careful. Its vines creep up houses and wrap around gutters. They're so heavy they pull them right off! As the plant gets bigger, so does the smell, so sickeningly sweet you could gag. Just another thing that starts off good and goes bad.

At the library, I pull open the heavy wooden doors and step inside the vestibule. Then, like I always do, I close my eyes and run my hands over the building's original brass doors that are propped open behind the wooden ones. Louise, the librarian, says they weigh two thousand pounds, and their decorations—an owl, a lion's paw, and fire—are symbols used by people long ago, before words even existed. They represent wisdom, power, and truth, "fragments of the poem of life," according to the library's architect, a guy named Solon Spencer Beman. Louise knows a ton of facts like that about the library, and since it was built in 1896, it's bursting with history. I imagine all that power and wisdom floating around the library, seeping into me like an amoeba doing its osmosis thing. My science teacher would be all over that.

Stepping into the library rotunda is like stepping through a magic portal. The roof is fifty feet high with a dome made of marble eight inches thick. Eight inches! I keep a list of Wisteria Library facts in Shoebox #2 and have memorized all of them. Details make a difference. You never know when an offbeat fact might come in handy.

Around the dome are portraits of New England authors like Harriett Beecher Stowe and Ralph Waldo Emerson. I love how they perch up there, keeping an eye out for us. Someday I'm going to write a novel, so I hope I'll magically absorb all the knowledge and wisdom those authors rain down on me.

I settle in with Hatshepsut (who happens to have been one of the few female Egyptian pharaohs and by far the most powerful) at my favorite table tucked into a corner behind the overstuffed chairs. I don't even get through a paragraph when it begins.

Noise. Not whispers. Regular voices.

"Move your queen to H four."

"If I do that, I expose my knight."

"Weigh your options."

The chess piece swooshes across the board and lands with a smack. I put my head on the table and close my eyes.

"Good choice."

Another swoosh. Then a pause. Sweet silence.

I go back to my book. Hatshepsut's journeys are fascinating.

"Oh no! Now what do I do?" one of them squeals.

"Sometimes you can't see ahead more than a couple of moves. You've gotta be ready for possible surprise attacks."

I plug my ears and close my eyes. *Relax. Breathe. Inhale for four, hold for seven, exhale for eight. Do it four times.* Mimi did yoga every day, even when she was sick. She taught me all about how to breathe through noise or tough feelings.

"Bishop to G two."

Only two breathwork cycles later, I turn and stare at a couple of teenage girls sitting at the other end of the bookshelves. They rake their eyes over the chessboard like they're mining diamonds.

I walk over to Louise at the librarian's desk. She and I hit it off from day one. Louise always makes sure I get the new books first, setting them aside before anyone else can read them, the pages impossibly crisp, the spines so tight and strict I don't want to ruin them by cracking them open and laying them flat. But I do. Every one of them.

Louise looks up and smiles. "Hello there, Jett."

"Hi, Louise." I fiddle with my silver bunny earring. "Yeah. So, there's a problem. The girls playing chess are so loud I can't read. I looked over at them a couple of times, but they won't quiet down."

"Jett, they aren't mind-readers. You need to speak to them, make a polite request."

"They're in high school. They won't listen to me." Nobody does.

Louise sighed. "Tell you what—"

Brrring!

Louise picks up the phone. "Wisteria Library, Louise here... Yes, of course, let me check." Louise punches something into her keyboard and scrolls down, obviously locating a requested book. Knowing this might take a while, I fire my frustration into courage, maybe just a small dose of it, but still, it's something, and whisper a quick prayer for help. Then I walk over to the girls.

"That's a mistake," one says, flipping her ponytail over her shoulder and pointing at the board.

I step closer to their table, clasping my hands behind my back. "Um. Excuse me?" I whisper.

Both girls are riveted to the board.

I clear my throat. "Excuse me." They look up. "I was wondering if you could be quieter since I'm trying to do my homework over there," I say, pointing to my table.

"Shouldn't you be doing your homework at *home*?" the girl with braces says, smiling tight so only a bit of the front wires showed.

"I like doing it here."

The other girl, Amelia, according to her notebook, points to the board. "About time you moved that pawn, Kit."

Kit picks up her pawn, then looks at me and says, "I'm a student too, you know. I have as much right to learning in this library as you do." She smacks her pawn down on a black square.

She has a point but… "The library is for, you know, quiet learning," I say.

Kit crosses her arms over her chest.

"I told you. Queen to H four would've prevented this scenario. Now you're gonna have to dig yourself out." Amelia shakes her head.

That makes two of us. I gather my stuff and move to another table. It doesn't seem right that they should get their way. They're ruining everything a person can count on when it comes to a library.

I glance over at Louise, her crisp button-down shirt tucked into the waist of a navy-blue skirt that just covers her knees. Shiny, flat brown shoes that look fresh out of the box. Her hair, a tight braid, not a strand out of place. Louise is so together. People listen to Louise. Nobody is going to push her around.

CHAPTER THREE

My stomach's grumbling, and I can't concentrate anyway, so I pack up my things and head home. Bad things come in threes, so that about does it for my Thursday. As I cross the street, the church bell rings, and I stretch my steps so they're in synch. My footsteps toll the bell five times. But when I look up at the huge white church steeple, I don't see any bell. Maybe it's one of those things that Mimi said you have to trust really exists, even though there isn't any physical evidence to prove it.

A nun's pulling weeds in the church garden. She's got a black veil on her head that covers her hair and makes a tight frame around her face. I wipe sweat from my forehead, happy I'm not all covered up in this heat.

The garden takes up most of the yard. There are at least fifteen rows of plants and flowers, evenly spaced and neatly trimmed. Perfect, peaceful order.

Along the back edge of the garden, rose bushes climb a tall white fence. On one side, sunflowers stand at attention like soldiers. A patch of daisies sway with the passing clouds. Wooden benches line all four sides of the garden as if they're giving it a big hug. Everything is totally content in a quiet, predictable, permanent place.

The nun waters the roses with a dented metal watering can, allowing each plant a five-second drink before moving on. I'm so in awe of the geometric perfection of that garden that I can't stop staring even though I know it's rude.

A plane drones. I shut my eyes and clap my hands over my ears until it passes and my stomach quiets.

When I open my eyes again, the nun's standing at the gate.

"Welcome!" she calls. "Come on in." She waves to me, her billowing black sleeve rippling from her pale arm like a flag in a breeze. I shake my head no. My parents would not be happy. They're against organized religion.

The nun keeps waving, and I chew the inside of my cheek, torn because I want to stand inside that magnificent garden... in silence. Fat chance. But for some reason, my hand reaches for the gate anyway, opens it, and inside I go.

The nun smiles and holds out her hand. "I'm Sister Gia. And you are...?"

I shake her hand. It feels dry and rough. Sister Gia smells like fresh-turned dirt.

"I'm Jett."

"Jet. Like the keys of a piano or a streak in the sky."

"Huh?"

"Jet black. Ebony. Or a jet airplane that flies so fast that it leaves a white trail behind it in the sky."

This nun isn't your typical religious type. She doesn't think in a straight line.

"I'm Jett with two t's. Short for Jeanette."

"Ah, I see. Do you like to garden, Jett?"

"I think I would. If I had a garden, that is."

She holds out the watering can. "Want to help?"

"Sure." I put my backpack on the bench and take the can. "Where should I begin?"

Sister Gia points to a row of cherry tomato plants. "They're pleading for water."

As I drizzle the tomatoes, a radio talk show streams from an old transistor tucked into the V of a tree branch.

"I'm Mr. Ed Dwayne, your host of SOSAD, the Safeguard Our Sons and Daughters show. We're opening up the lines today for your questions in response to our topic, a listener-favorite: shaping our children's behavior. My guest, Dr. Brendan Bullock, is here to answer your questions, so give us a call at 867-2501."

I tune out Mr. Ed. His kid, Lars, is in my class, and Mr. Ed has chaperoned a field trip or two. A know-it-all. Never lets his son finish a sentence.

Sister Gia turns off the radio, then pulls a tissue from her skirt waist and dabs at her forehead.

"Isn't your headpiece awful hot?" I ask.

"Oh, I'm used to it by now. Going on twenty-five years."

I give the plants one last sprinkle and put down the watering can. "You must've been young when you joined the convent. I mean, you don't look ancient." Argh. I'm always surprised how my words have a mind of their own.

Sister Gia closes her eyes and mumbles numbers. "No, you're right. Right as God's rain. I was only eighteen when I joined. Nowadays, in our order, a girl needs to be twenty-one years old to commit. Good thing, too. Teenagers aren't known for rational thinking."

Next to the tomatoes, rows of herb plants line up behind popsicle sticks with their names printed in black magic marker.

"How did you get the garden to grow so perfectly?" I ask.

"Lots of attention. Daily weeding and watering. After that, it's just a matter of letting plants do what they need to do. A botanical give and take." She picks up the shears and snips at the rose bushes. "Put on those gloves, and you can help by picking up these sappers and putting them in the basket. Save me a few steps."

A grey cat slinks out from behind a pine tree and sits on Sister G's foot. He's a big guy, and he only has one ear.

"Hello, Grey Cat," Sister says, reaching down to scratch his head. "I'll fill your food bowl as soon as I finish up here."

"What happened to his ear?"

"Not sure. He showed up here looking like that. Don't let it fool you, though. Grey Cat doesn't miss a trick. It's called compensation. He may not hear well, but his sight and sense of smell are one hundred and ten percent. He reports everything that goes on in this garden to me. And he's not our only inhabitant with such unique attributes."

Sister goes back to work, trimming the roses easily as if they didn't even have thorns that could draw blood. She takes her time, examines each branch, whispers something to it before cutting. "Always snip, don't yank," she tells me. "We don't want to upset their souls." The scene feels like a dream.

Ignoring my stomach grumbles, I slip on the brown gloves.

"Souls?" I ask. "Roses have souls?"

"Certainly. Every living thing embodies a soul. Every soul needs to be protected."

I survey the garden, imagining every plant, flower, and herb with faces and something to say. More like a cartoon than reality.

"What's it like to be a nun?"

The church fascinates me. My parents say it's a male-dominated hierarchy that abuses its power. Which, of course, makes me even more interested in this nun, a woman who seems perfectly happy, and not like a victim at all.

"We're up for morning prayers by five-thirty. Then at seven, we eat breakfast. For the rest of the morning, we do different things, depending on what our responsibility is. Me, I chose to maintain the grounds. At one o'clock, it's lunchtime. Dinner's at six."

"Does everyone obey the schedule? I mean, they have to, right?"

"Yes. It's what we all signed on for."

Like a promise.

I look up into the sky and remember my promise to my grandmother to always strive to make and keep peace. Life at the convent seems peaceful.

When the basket is just about full of clipped branches, Sister Gia puts her shears on top of them and steps back to assess the bushes. She nods at the roses and says, "Now give me some more of your brilliant blooms, my lovelies!"

She picks up the basket and turns to me. "Would you care to join us for supper? Sister Theresa made a Greek salad with cukes and tomatoes straight from this garden, then garnished it with basil from right over there." She points to a large plant. "Grateful to you, my fragrant friend!" she calls.

I take off the gloves and hand them to her. "Thank you, but my mother's expecting me for dinner at home."

Doubtful. My family doesn't have a set dinner time and we each mostly eat on our own. "But would it be okay if I came back tomorrow?"

"I'll be here as usual." Sister G brushes some grass off her skirt and leans down to pick up Grey Cat's food bowl. A book with a pen clipped to its cover pokes out of the side pocket of Sister's skirt. She pushes it back in, but the silver pen falls to the ground. I pick it up and strain to read the engraving. *RTD*. Someone's initials. Obviously not the nun's.

Sister takes the pen from me and sticks it back in her pocket.

"Thanks. My notebook and pen have a life all their own, always trying to flee my habit and see the big world."

"Habit?"

Sister G pats her skirt and top. "This is called my habit. I wear it habitually," she says with a wink.

I nod, my eyes still on the nun's pocket. "That looks like a pretty fancy notebook," I say. "The binding and all."

Sister G reaches back into her pocket and removes the book. It's small, about the size of the framed picture of me and my twin brothers that sits on the mantel in our living room. The spine of the book is bright red, and the front and back cover look like the black and white checked fabric of a pair of pants my mom hemmed for a neighbor the other day.

"Just one of my home-made journals. I've always enjoyed book-making," she says, watching a bee land on her arm. "It's a nice creative outlet. Besides writing, that is." She smiles at the bee, and it buzzes off into a lilac bush.

Wow. Maybe nuns have special powers over things with souls.

"I like to write too," I tell her. "I'm going to be an author and write long novels. Epics. I've already got lists of story ideas. My friend and I are actually writing a graphic novel now."

"Wonderful! Books are the mirrors of the soul." Sister G runs her hand over the fabric cover. "Virginia Woolf."

"Mirrors?"

"It's a metaphor. It means writers tap into their innermost thoughts and feelings when writing their stories."

I nod and point at Sister G's journal. "What's yours about?"

I cover my mouth with my hand. Something's come over me in this garden. Usually, I'd rather write than talk. It's easier, and I can plan it out first. With talking, I never can predict what'll come out of my mouth. But there's something about the nun, about her garden, something familiar that invites me in, in a way I can't refuse.

Sister Gia runs her finger up and down the red taped spine for forever. Finally, she says, "I write lots of things. Poems, recipes, stories." She blinks twice and puts the book back into her pocket. "I pray every day. I write every day. It's all just part of my schedule."

Sister's life sounds as healthy and delicious as the turkey noodle soup Mimi used to make every year, the day after Thanksgiving. Maybe I'll be an author and a nun.

"Well, I'll see you tomorrow," I say.

Sister loops the basket of thorny twigs over her arm, places Grey Cat's bowl on top, and turns toward the church.

"I hope so. This garden's frantic for fertilizer. I've got compost waiting, and it's much more fun sharing the job with another."

Sister G slips inside the side door of the little house behind the church, and Grey Cat scampers off toward the back of the garden, through the slats of the white fence. I practically skip through the garden to the gate, thrilled that I've discovered the very lifestyle I've been searching for. Not that I'm ready to join a nunnery. I just want to live inside of a nice, comfy schedule. Somewhere with no room for surprises. Or loud voices I'd rather forget.

CHAPTER FOUR

As soon as I get home, I let Felix out of his cage for his fifteen minutes of exercise and grab my journal from my desk drawer. It's not as pretty as Sister G's, but it'll do. On a clean page, I write the date and list my plans.

TO-DO LIST #134—GETTING PEACE
1. Organize desk
2. Organize clothes closet
3. Make a calendar schedule for each day, including weekends
4. Make a calendar schedule for the family, including mealtimes
5. Keep lists of what works and what doesn't for future organizing

I line up my stuffed animals on my bed, straighten my desk, and put all the pens in the cup, pointing the same way. In the closet, I space each of the hangers a half-inch apart. (Measuring tapes are my friends.) I brush down the sleeves of the shirts with my hand, making sure none of them stick out, line them up like soldiers in a parade. Tomorrow I'll weed out the closet and take any extras to Goodwill. If Sister G wears the same outfit every day, then I surely don't need twelve tee-shirts or more than a couple of pairs of shorts.

Next, I tidy up the bookshelves and organize the books by genre, one section for mysteries, one for fiction, one for non-fiction. I group all the covers by color, each shelf a ribbon of rainbow.

I give my matryoshka dolls their own separate shelf, placing each on a tiny x marked in pencil, one inch apart, to keep watch over the bedroom.

Scritch-scratch-scritch.

"Felix, no!" My bunny is munching the corner off of my Hatshepsut book. "That'll make you sick." I scoop him up and put him back in his cage. "We need to follow your schedule exactly, Felix. It's been over fifteen minutes. My bad. From now on, I'll let you out from three to three-fifteen pm each day before I head to the library, and I'll keep a better eye on you. At three-fifteen sharp, I'll leave for the library, then come back and feed you a cup of lettuce at five-thirty. While you eat, I'll organize my bedroom. How does that sound?"

Felix just nuzzles the wire cage, as if wondering why he'd lost his freedom.

"It's the best way, trust me," I tell him.

I find a bowl of tuna salad and a handful of baby carrots in the fridge. As I wait for a tortilla to warm in the microwave, my brothers play in the backyard, shrieking about Spider Man. My parents are on the porch watching them. The squeaky glider gives them away.

Just as I finish putting my food on a plate, Mom comes in and rummages around in the cupboard. "You're eating early today," she says as she pulls out a box of crackers. "Your trip into town must have made you hungry."

"Nope. I'm just on a new schedule."

"Since when do we do schedules around here?" Mom crinkles her forehead.

"Since I can never count on anything."

"One thing you can always count on is cheese and crackers before dinner," Dad says as he opens the refrigerator door. Mom hands him a sleeve of crackers. I roll my eyes.

"Jett, you're not still upset that we adopted Felix instead of that cat?" she asks me. "Goodness, it's been weeks, and the bunny lives in your room."

"That day at the animal shelter is a perfect example of the way this family works. We went in to adopt a black and white tabby, and we came out with a rabbit. Can't count on anything."

"Felix is darling. And much easier than a cat."

"You know I love Felix. But plans aren't made to be broken." I look at my watch. "Gotta go."

"Here, give the Gouda a go before you go." Dad chuckles at his corny joke, as usual. He holds out a cracker with orange cheese on it and pats the chair next to his at the table.

I grab my plate. "No thanks. Felix gets his greens at exactly five-thirty."

Mom eyes the watch I'd just started wearing again that afternoon. My parents don't believe in watches. They like to look at the sun and estimate the time. Most of the time they're pretty accurate too. But precision is important, so the watch.

I head to my room to complete my list of chores while I eat. Right on schedule. Felix is counting on me.

•   •   •

The next day, I tape the family schedule up on the refrigerator. Fifteen minutes later, Bo bursts into my room waving it above his head.

"No way, Jett! Are you serious? We aren't gonna do this. It's boring." He balls up the schedule and shoots it into the wastebasket.

I pull it out and flatten it on my desk. "You should be thanking me. You'll never miss any of your TV shows because of late dinners. You can make play dates with your friends because you'll know exactly how much free time you have in the afternoons. What's not to like?"

He stomps out of the room. "Mom! Jett's acting like a jerk."

"What's up with this supposed schedule, Jett?" Dad asks, as he and Mom enter and look over my shoulder at the wrinkled page. Bo and Jack stand at the door, eager to witness a show-down.

I point to the next day's morning activities. "It'll work out great. We can all eat breakfast at seven. I'll even volunteer to cook tomorrow. Pancakes. You guys would love that, right?" I smile at them, and they scowl. "After school, we take a quick break for a snack—"

"Whoa now! Whatever happened to the idea of democracy?" Mom asks.

"I'm just exercising my right to free speech," I counter.

"It'll never stand up to the test of time," Dad says. He evaluates ideas like he does buildings.

"We're a family," Mom chimes in. "We talk things out. We need to agree—"

"We never all agree," I say.

Dad shakes his head. "Majority rules, Jett."

I tug at my earring. The ache feels good. "I'm always in the minority. It's like I'm not even a part of this family."

"Of course you are, Jett." Mom puts her arm around my shoulders. "You just need to learn to be more flexible, listen to others."

I shrug her arm away. "The only one who ever listened to me was Mimi." I bite my lower lip and turn away.

Silence.

Dad speaks in a low tone. "Mimi wouldn't like rules imposed on her either."

I turn back toward them. Bo and Jack are still leaning against the bedroom door, grinning like they'd already won the fight. Mom and Dad just look at me the way they looked at Felix when they first saw him at the animal shelter. With pity.

Dad picks up the schedule.

"Schedules don't work for us, Jett. They're too rigid. Flexibility is a great trait to acquire."

I stand, my fingernails digging into my fists. "If we used schedules, then maybe Mimi might still be alive today." I glare at them, daring anyone to say anything.

Mom does. "Mimi had a heart attack. A schedule wouldn't have helped."

"I asked you to list everything I needed to do for her while you were away, and you said it wasn't necessary." My teeth grind even though I'm not telling them to. "If I'd had a schedule telling me when to give her the pain medicine, it might not have happened."

"Jett, her pain meds wouldn't have kept her alive."

"You don't know that! Her heart could have stopped because she was in so much pain."

"The doctors said—"

I hold my fists up in front of my face and shake them. "Who cares about the doctors! While you were looking at Open Houses, I was taking care of her. She died on my watch!" I push the chair and it takes off, rolling smack into my desk.

Now the twins' faces are as white as Felix's tummy.

"Please," I say. "Get out."

"Jett, it wasn't your fault."

"Then whose fault was it?" I scour their faces for an answer, even though I know what it is.

Mom shakes her head and leaves the room, followed by Dad and Bo and Jack. Predictable. The few predictable things in my life, unfortunately, are not good.

"Why won't you talk about it with me?" I scream. They keep on walking.

I slam the door and pick up my matryoshka. "Mimi? What do you do when people go silent on you?" I hold the doll to my ear and wait for an answer.

CHAPTER FIVE

Thellie and I walk to and from school together every day. Sometimes, if I walk fast enough, my world quiets down, but not usually on a school day. Not usually with Thellie.

"Jett, want to come to my house later?" Thellie skips to keep up with me. "We can work on our graphic novel. Only three pages left, and we're done! Then we work on marketing. My dad said he'll help us draw up a business plan. This is getting so official!"

I love going to Thellie's house. When we work on our book, the only sound is Thellie's mother setting the table for dinner. The gentle clicks as she sets the silverware down on the polished wood table. Spoons tapping on pots in the kitchen. The promise of delicious in more ways than one. Thellie's is a normal family, just her and her parents, eating together every day. Not only that, they also have quiet time at night, sort of like adult swim at the pool. From seven to nine, everything stops. No TV or talking. Everybody does their own thing, whether they read or draw or study. Thellie complains that two hours of quiet time daily is too much, but I'm pretty sure that's how she got to be such a great artist.

"I'll come tomorrow, Thellie. Today I have things I have to do."

"Aw, come on, Jett. We're getting so close." Thellie slows to a walk. She holds her thumb and pointer finger about an inch apart and squints her eyes. "This close, Jett. A complete graphic novel. We'll officially be authors!"

"I'm sorry, I can't. But tomorrow, I promise."

Thellie gives a weak wave and turns into her driveway. When I get home, I change my clothes, tend to my Felix To-Do List, and then run to the church as if pulled by a magnet.

Sister G's at the far end of the garden clipping peonies. She holds up each flower and examines it, then hands it to me gently, as if it were destined to be part of some fancy bouquet.

I sniff a peony. "If you don't pick flowers at just the right time—on schedule—they might die before you have a chance to show them off indoors, right?"

"I suppose that's a fair assessment."

Confirmed. Flowers and humans all need schedules.

"You guys—er, nuns—believe in heaven, right?"

"We strive to live a proper life here on earth so we can rest in peace in heaven."

"My parents don't believe in heaven. They aren't religious."

Sister puts down her shears and brushes off her black sleeves. "Everyone is entitled to their own beliefs." She walks toward the hedges, and I follow her.

"My Mimi didn't go to church a lot, but she prayed and believed in God. Do you think that's good enough to get her into heaven?"

"What do your parents have to say about that?" Sister strolls the paths, running her hands along the tops of the hedges, ruffling them like Mom does with my brothers' hair, mumbling something now and then.

"They think the soul moves on to the next life, maybe even inside a different body, like a bird or a fish. I bet my Mimi would've loved to have been a bird."

"That's a comforting thought." Grey Cat slinks from under the bushes and lays down by Sister's foot, then rolls onto his back. Sister gives him a scratch and then fills a bowl with water that Grey Cat laps up fast.

"But isn't there some scientific theory that tells what happens when a person dies?"

"I'm not the one to ask that question. I'm as far from a scientist as they come." She sits on the bench. "Sounds like your Mimi was your dear friend."

I sit down next to her. "She was. The best. But I wasn't to her. In the end, at least." I pick at a thread hanging from my shorts. "She had a heart attack while

I was taking care of her." Sister Gia turns and faces me head-on. "My parents didn't leave a schedule for her meds. They didn't tell me to give her any medicine while they were gone."

"Some things are out of our control, Jett."

"I can at least try to keep things in control. If only I knew what to do."

The garden gate squeaks, and another nun enters.

"Sister Patrice!" Sister G calls, waving her over. "Welcome."

Sister Patrice looks around in all directions before striding briskly to the bench as if time were running out.

"Jett, this is a friend of mine. Sister Patrice is in charge of the church choir. She was born singing and hasn't stopped since!"

Sister Patrice nods and gives me the once-over.

"The usual?" Sister G asks her.

"Yes, please," Patrice whispers.

Sister G picks a handful of herbs and hands them to Sister Patrice. "Your throat feeling any better?"

"A bit. Not enough to sing."

"Hmmm... It's been three days." Sister G goes back over to the herbs and picks a leaf from a bush near the back. She cups it in her palm and whispers something to it. Then she hands it to her friend.

"Use this sparingly. It's stronger than the others. Steep it in hot water with the juice of one lemon."

"Thank you. Please pray for me." Sister Patrice leaves, the gate clanking closed behind her.

"What was that all about? Are you some kind of healer?"

Smiling, Sister G pulls out her fancy notebook. "I've got many tinctures and herbal recipes here created by my mother and her mother before her. Splendid concoctions. That said, I'm not sure why Sister Patrice isn't better yet." She scrunches her eyes and leans forward. "The herbs are doing well, really flourishing, so they should be effective." A monarch butterfly lifts off from a daisy and settles onto Sister's shoulder. She's a regular Dr. Doolittle.

"Wait. Why doesn't she just pray to get better?"

"Prayer is good, but it's even better in combination with nature. Sometimes a person needs to rise up and take action."

"I prayed my grandmother would survive, but she didn't. I pray for quiet in my house and at school but never get it. I pray for the headaches to go away, but they don't. It would be great if there were a person in the sky who could fix my broken life. If there is, they don't hear me."

Sister G scrunches up her eyes. "Headaches?"

"Sometimes loud sounds make my head hurt. And sometimes my head hurts for no reason." I gaze around the garden. "Do you think there's something in your garden that could cure my headaches?"

"Do your parents know about your headaches, Jett?"

"Mom says maybe it's hormones. She says I'm at 'that age'."

"She may very well be right. And if your mother says it's okay, then I'd be glad to whip up a tincture for your headaches."

I frown and shrug. That conversation won't be happening because Mom would never approve of my new friend.

"And how is your life broken?" Sister G asks.

"Feels that way. Something's missing. Peace, for one thing."

Sister nods. "How can one find peace?"

"I don't know! These voices in my head—" I clap my hand over my mouth. Now I've done it. She'll call my parents and they'll have me institutionalized.

"Go on," she urges. "Maybe I can help."

"You can't tell anyone. Only my Mimi knows." Maybe nuns make a contract with God to keep people's secrets, since it's the kind thing to do.

"Everyone holds conversations in their head. It's how we work things out."

I take a deep breath and the scents from Sister G's herbs fill my lungs. "The voices are loud and... and they scare me." Ugh. Why am I talking so much to a woman I hardly know?

"What are these voices saying, Jett?"

I shake my head. "Never mind." Grey Cat slinks through the fence and I wish I could follow him.

Sister G opens her notebook and jots something down. "There's a book you might like to read. Might help you feel better, more peaceful."

"Like a medical or self-help book?"

Sister laughs. "Not a medical book. Interpreted a certain way, it could be considered self-help. But it's fiction. A novel about a girl your age. Look for it at the library next time you go."

"You think it'd help me fix my life?" Just what I need. No unanswered prayers involved.

She smiles. "I'm afraid lives don't work like that. Can't just put a big old band-aid on them and assume they'll heal. Takes a little more than that."

Sister tears out the page and gives it to me.

Resurrecting the Dragon by S. A. Rahdear.

"What does the S.A. stand for?"

"There's no author information in the book."

"So, it's a fairy tale?" I'm too old for fairy tales, and I'm not into dragons.

"Not exactly."

"But it's about a dragon."

"In this case, the dragon is metaphorical."

I roll my eyes. "So, the dragon stands for something else."

"Yes. In ancient times, people believed dragons protected treasures by breathing fire, and soldiers would fight a dragon to get the goods. Dragons have a good side and a scary side, depending on to whom you're talking."

"Like whether you're the soldier who wants the treasure or the owner of the treasure who hired the dragons?"

"Yes, one could look at it that way. But different cultures see dragons in different ways. I prefer the

Chinese interpretation. They believe dragons are lucky and symbolize power and good fortune."

"*Resurrecting the Dragon*. So, it's a story about a dead dragon who comes back to life?"

Sister G laughs. "Read it. You'll see."

I fold up the paper into a tiny square. "It sounds mysterious. If the book's as hard to understand as its title, maybe it's not for me."

Sister G stands. "Give the book a chance. Even if you don't care for it, you'll learn something worthwhile from it. That's the way books are."

I'd failed at peace so far, so what harm could reading the book do?

• • •

At the library, I do a computer search to find *Resurrecting the Dragon*, and it finally comes up under middle-grade. One copy is available. Not a long book. Good. The quicker I can read it, the faster the voices in my head will disappear.

In a few weeks the library renovation will begin, and the shelves have already been moved around, so the middle-grade fiction section is temporarily located in the basement, along with non-fiction kid books.

At the bottom of the pink granite stairs, in the basement, the lights on the walls flicker every so often like they do when there's a terrible thunderstorm. I walk on tiptoe on the bare concrete floor to keep my flip-flops from smacking, even though it feels like I'm the only one down here. I find the shelf with the book's call number and pull it down.

The corners of the black cover are curling. On the front, a gold dragon exhales the title, *Resurrecting the Dragon*, in a burst of orange flames. I flip through the pages. A few have illustrations. But at the start of Chapter One, someone's scribbled all over the page with black marker. I can only decipher bits of letters, no words, and definitely no sentences. Annoying because it's a middle-grade book, not a toddler book. Older kids should've grown out of doing such stupid things.

The next page is no better. Black marker hides every word, so I flip to the first page that isn't marked up. An illustration. A girl in a forest. Trees with branches reaching out like arms, some clasped together as if in prayer. The girl reaches her arms out also as if she's carrying on a conversation with the trees. I turn the page to find out what she's saying, but someone has torn it out. That one, and the five pages after it.

I flip to the end of the book to look for clues. There's the girl again, looking like she's been through a tough time, her dress stained and ragged at the hem. But she stands strong in a gigantic garden full of sunflowers and her hands spew fire as she points at a pile of ash. The quote under the illustration says, "Swiha! I will be silent no longer!" My nose tickles, and I swear I smell autumn leaves even though it's spring. My ears buzz and my head throbs.

Shhh!

Dizzy, I slap the book shut, palms sticky on the cover. Sweat forms on my forehead despite my arms being so chilly that the hair on them is standing up. What kind of power does that girl have? And are those the ashes of the dragon?

Now my arms tingle, and my biceps twitch just like they did after Jessica Callahan told me I looked like a boy when I got my hair cut short. I'm not a fighter, but that day I would've knocked Jessica all the way to Canada if Thellie hadn't stopped me.

A grunt from the other side of the room brings me back, and I set the book back on the shelf. I slink along close to the bookcases, following the sound over to the corner by the non-fiction books. I peek around the edge of the shelf. A woman is curled up on the floor under a beach towel with pinwheels printed on it. She's wearing a beanie cap pulled down low over her eyes. Her gray ponytail streams down her back. A gauzy long dress covers her where the beach towel doesn't, and she has on scuffed army boots, untied. A tiny kitten dozes in the crook of her arm.

I know this woman. Her name is Adeline. On rainy days, Adeline sits upstairs by the fireplace reading the newspaper or a magazine. She never speaks to anybody. Louise told me that Adeline had taken a fall and hit her head so hard that she went into a coma. When she woke up a few hours later, her voice was different, and she spoke with a French accent. It's a thing called foreign accent syndrome, and it totally embarrassed Adeline, so she stopped talking altogether. If she needs to ask the librarians a question, she writes it down in a notebook so people won't laugh at her.

Adeline starts snoring and rolls over on her side, nuzzling into a huge transparent shopping bag stuffed with clothes, a bag of kitty kibbles, a thermos, a hairbrush, and some other items I can't make out. I worry she doesn't have anywhere else to go. Here I am complaining of living in too many homes while this woman might not even have one. Adeline and the kitten look comfortable, so I let her be and go back for the book.

It's gone.

I check the label on the shelf and confirm I'm in the right spot, but the book is not here.

I go back upstairs. Louise is sitting at her desk, pecking at her computer keyboard.

"Jett! Perfect timing. The third Theodosia book has been returned. I know you want to reread it before the new one comes out." She pulls it from a drawer and hands it to me.

I run my hand over the glossy cover. The Theodosia Throckmorton series by R. L. LaFevers. Theo's a kid sleuth who solves ancient mysteries, and I'd give anything to have her patient mind even when things get scary.

"Thanks, Louise."

Then I hand her the slip of paper from Sister G, with the book's title and author.

"I was reading this book downstairs, but now it's disappeared. Did somebody just check it out?"

Louise looks hard at the paper like it's written in Latin.

"Hmmm... No." She hands the note back to me and begins to sort the books on her desk.

"I only walked away from it for a minute and when I got back, it was gone."

"It's possible someone put it back on the shelf," Louise says.

"I checked. Not there."

"Maybe someone put it on the wrong shelf."

"No. I looked all over. Plus, I was the only one down there. I think." I shuffle my feet as if to erase my little white lie. There might be a rule against sleeping on the basement floor, but Adeline may have nowhere else to sleep.

"Do you think you could get the book for me from another library? Sister Gia told me about it, and I really want to read it."

Louise stops sorting. "Sister Gia?" She fingers the cross that hangs from a chain around her neck and shakes her head. "She recommended that book?"

"Why wouldn't she?"

Louise goes back to the books. She clears her throat. "It's a bit... well... unconventional."

"What do you mean?"

Louise pushes her glasses up her nose and keeps sorting. "Just not the type of book that would be popular in this town, that's all."

"Why not? It has some pretty cool illustrations in it. A girl with magical powers and trees that look human because they're pointing and praying. But somebody marked up the pages, so I'm not sure what it all means."

I expect Louise to be alarmed to hear a book has been mistreated, but she doesn't flinch.

"Please, Louise, can you get me the book from another library?"

"I'm afraid they've disappeared as well." She stacks two more books in a pile.

"All of them? Why?"

"Not sure. People borrow books from the library all the time and never return them."

"But how can you be sure they're gone without looking them up?"

Louise wrinkles up her nose like she smells something bad. "I know the book. It's missing. Not a copy left."

"But there is a copy left because I read some of it downstairs."

"Chances are slim to none that it'll reappear."

"What are the chances that all copies of one book disappear? You said people around here wouldn't like the book. So why check it out in the first place, let alone not return it?"

She shrugs and picks up a book with a frayed cover, runs her thumb along the spine. "Hmmm... Excuse me while I find the tape."

Louise usually treats me special, but today she's treating me like a missing book. Invisible.

CHAPTER SIX

As we pass the library on our way to school, I ask Thellie what she thinks about Louise.

"She's a librarian, so she's probably smart?"

"Right. Got that. Go deeper. Has she ever... well... acted weird around you?"

Thellie searches my face for a third eye. "She's only done librarian stuff around me, Jett. I can't say much more about her."

I don't mind that Thellie and I aren't always on the same wavelength. Soon enough I'll be moving again, so I'm better off not getting too close.

"Anyway," Thellie continues, "I'm only at the library once or twice a month when I need to do research for school or something."

"I go every day now. Nice and quiet there. Usually."

"Every day! Doesn't that get boring?"

"Nope. The library is full of a zillion un-boring things." And across the street is The Most Un-Boring Person I've ever met. But that's secret information.

"So, what's so unusual about Louise, anyway?" Thellie asks.

"Did you ever feel like you knew somebody and then one day something happens that makes you feel like you don't really know them at all?"

Thellie switches her backpack to her other shoulder and begins to hum, a sign that she's thinking or nervous, like during a test, or when people argue.

"Well… Sometimes my mom gets in a horrible mood where she hardly says a word to me or Dad. I can't ever figure out what makes her go silent like that, but I don't ask her because she gets mad when I do."

"Your mom? Your mom is always happy and talkative when I see her."

Thellie rolls her eyes and shakes her head. "Believe me, she's not always. Sometimes the quiet at my house hurts my ears."

"Come to my house when that happens. Guaranteed to solve your problem. You'll be craving quiet time by the time you leave."

Thellie forces a smile and starts humming a song from the play, *Wicked.*

I pull open the front door and we enter Wisteria Middle School. Grades six through eight are in this building, and seventh grade couldn't arrive soon enough for me. I won't be at the bottom of the social ladder anymore. I'll still be low but not the lowest, as long as we don't move before then. And that's a big "if." Being new at school automatically puts you at the bottom of the ladder, no matter what grade you're in. I've already made room in my brain for another ending. I'm a pro at making room for endings.

We make our way to homeroom and settle into our desks next to each other in the back row. An intense discussion about a movie about the end of the world is going on in front of us. A couple of girls braid each other's hair while the boys next to them watch.

"Ahem! Attention up here, please," Mr. Clayburn says, pointing to the screen on the wall.

"Good morning, students, and welcome to Wonderful Wednesday! The only announcement I have for you today is that because of this beautiful late spring weather, you have permission to eat lunch outside! The cafeteria will be closed except for purchasing your food. But when outside, please stay in the table area on the terrace or at the edge of the field so you can hear the bell when it rings. Now do good work and get out there and catch the crest!"

Mrs. Montak, assistant principal, is probably an ex-surfer. Kids roll their eyes when she says things like, "Don't fight the waves, ride 'em!" or "If you find yourself in rough water, paddle toward shore and take a breather," or "You can't change the tides so you might as well go with the flow." An Eternal Optimist.

After the announcement, everybody whoops and cheers. Not me. Too many run-ins with ants and bees have turned me off to picnics and other outdoor meals. My plan is to eat fast and go back inside to talk to the cafeteria ladies. Those ladies have kitchen organization down to a science, down to the very last spoon. I always learn a thing or two from them.

Lunch comes way too soon. Thellie and I unwrap our sandwiches at a picnic table, and Rodney plunks down on the bench.

"Hey, Jett," he says, smiling. "Oh. And hey, Thell," he says as an afterthought.

Thellie claims Rodney likes me, and I'm beginning to agree, seeing as he has a habit of looking at me without saying much.

"Hi, Rodney, what's up?"

Rod unwraps a ginormous sandwich that drips oil and bits of black olives onto the table. He grabs a napkin and tries to mop it all up but only manages to mush it into the wood, leaving a dark blotch that's extremely unappetizing. And a perfect oasis for ants.

"After we eat, I want to show you the plans for my new robot. It's amazing." He takes an overambitious bite of his sandwich and, realizing it's too big, holds his hand in front of his mouth till he reduces it to a more manageable size.

I look at Thellie who's frowning at the tuna sandwich her mom packed for her.

"Not hungry?" I ask.

"I'm just tired of tuna. Mondays and Wednesdays are no-meat days in our house and it's boooor-ing."

I tear my ham sandwich into quarters and give her a piece.

Thellie bites into it and closes her eyes, savoring as if it were straight off some fancy restaurant menu. "Thanks. I love the honey mustard your mom uses." I hand her another piece.

After a bite or two, I bunch up my trash, grab my bag, and stand, ready to make an exit before bees get a whiff of Rod's apple juice.

"Sit down, Jett. We still have another fifteen minutes," Rodney says. "Here, have a peach."

"No, no thanks, Rod, I'm—"

A jet flies overhead, drowning out the buzz on the school terrace. I drop my stuff on the table and cover my ears. It creeps across the sky, slower than ants carrying crumbs to an anthill. I try to catch my breath but can't. Panicked, I sprint toward the door, but as I enter the cafeteria, I run into a garbage can and fall. The linoleum floor smells like pine cleaner, and my stomach cramps.

"Jett! You okay?" Thellie grabs my arm and helps me up.

I bend over the garbage can and throw up. Thellie backs away and hums "You're a Good Man, Charlie Brown."

Laughter rushes in from the lunch terrace.

I hear Rodney shout, "Shut up, you guys! It's not funny. Cut it out!"

The laughter continues and suddenly Rodney is at my side with my bag. Mrs. Langley leans over and hands me a warm washcloth to wipe off my mouth.

"Thanks," I say. "I—I don't know what happened."

"No worries." Mrs. Langley hands Rod a hall pass. "Take her to the nurse, would you, dear?"

He nods, and I follow him and Thellie into the hall.

"I'm not going to the nurse. I'll stop at the restroom and rinse my mouth. Then I'll meet you in the library."

"You sure?" he asks. "Maybe you should have the nurse take your temperature."

"Rod, I'll be fine."

In the restroom, I take off my shoe and wedge it under the door so nobody can get in this time. I look at my marks on the stall wall. Seems like I just put the eighth one up there. I grit my teeth and reach up to scratch the ninth tally this month into the wall. I'm now about six inches from the corner and running out of room.

It's a big joke that Jett hates jets. Their noise is almost as bad as the voices. I cup my hands and take a drink of water from the sink, swishing it around and spitting it out to freshen up my mouth. I splash water on my face, but it only makes my head ache more. The bell rings and my time is up.

In the library, Rod spreads out his sketches. "Your ears still hurt, Jett?" He takes a long time spacing his papers just right.

Thellie puts her hand on my arm. "Maybe you should talk to your mom. Maybe a doctor should check your ears."

I shake my head. "No. Not necessary. I told you. I have hyperacusis, over-sensitivity to sounds. Believe me, it's a thing."

Rod clears his throat. "But you were fine in the theater during the Star Wars movie."

"It's only certain noises. Ones that surprise me. I'm familiar with Star Wars sounds."

"Aren't you pretty familiar with the sound of airplanes, too?" Thellie asks gently.

I roll my eyes. "Of course. Just every so often, they make my stomach feel funny. You know, they're so loud." I lean over to see one of Rod's sketches better. "So, what will this robot do?"

The diversion works, and Rodney points out all the cool features of his robot. Thellie's eyes wander. Technology isn't her thing.

"This guy'll be able to use his arms like a human, but he'll never get tired. He'll be able to work on an assembly line forever. Not that I'd have him do that, of course."

"I bet he'd make a great hitman," I say.

My two friends look at me like I'd grown antlers. Thellie hums "Tomorrow" from the Broadway show, *Annie.*

"Hitman?" Rod asks. "Now, why would I need him to do that?"

"I'm just saying that he could be used for self-defense. Take care of bullies and other evil people."

Rodney folds up his sketches. "What's going on, Jett?"

I shake my head and pick up my backpack.

"Seriously, I'm starting to worry about you."

"Worrying is for mothers, Rod, so quit doing it."

"Those kids who laughed at you are weak," he says. "They hurt your feelings, but they didn't touch you."

"You never know when mean words will turn into something else."

Thellie squints at me like she's got double vision.

"Is somebody bothering you, Jett?" Rod asks. "I need to know. Maybe I can help."

I glare at him. "Rodney. No."

He shrugs and zips up his backpack. "See you after school, then," he says and exits the library.

Thellie stands. "Remember when you asked me if I knew anybody who suddenly acted like someone else?" I avoided her eyes. "Sometimes *you* do these days, Jett. And it makes me sadder than when my mom won't talk."

"Everybody has a bad day once in a while, Thell. I'm fine."

"It's not just a bad day, Jett. You haven't been yourself for weeks. You should let your friends help. Or at least try to. But we can't if you won't talk to us about stuff."

"There's nothing to talk about."

The echo of bouncing basketballs and kids yelling in the gym is close now. I wish we could do solitary sports in PE, like track or weight-lifting.

Thellie pulls open the door to the girls' locker room and goes in. I slump against the wall. Two girls walk by and point at me and snicker.

"What's your problem?" I mutter under my breath.

The girls hold out their arms as if ready for take-off. "Whooosh!" one says, and they fly down the hall.

I need to get my hands on that book. *Resurrecting the Dragon* is the only way I'd learn how to ride the waves instead of fighting them.

CHAPTER SEVEN

I'm here ready to work in the garden, but Sister Gia isn't. The place looks so ordinary without her. Grey Cat is absent, and not one bee is buzzing.

I check the church. When I open the door, the smell of candle wax and incense greets me, all cool and musty. The dimly lit space and the soft air muffle any sound that tries to trickle in.

Sister G is kneeling in a front pew, hands folded, head bowed. She whispers something to herself as she fiddles with a string of beads. Finally, she looks up and sees me. She touches her forehead, chest, left side, right side, and says, "Amen."

"You're here a bit early today, Jett. No library?"

I sit next to her. "Not much homework today."

Sister goes back to her beads, and I watch her click-clack them between her fingers. "Can you make wishes with those?" I ask.

Sister chuckles. "You say prayers with rosary beads. I suppose prayers are a bit like wishes."

"Who are you praying for?"

"Everyone who needs it. Everyone I know. Or knew."

I pull out a book from the rack on the back of the pew in front of me and open it. A songbook. An organ sits on the raised floor in front that reminds me of a theater stage. I shudder at the idea of songs and organ pipes blasting through this place that's so perfectly quiet.

"Well, if I had those beads, I'd pray for answers to all my mysteries."

Sister hands the beads to me and looks me in the eye. "Mysteries?"

"Yup. And one of them is me."

"What question about you needs answering?"

I shrug.

"You feeling tousled?"

"Huh?" I roll the beads between my fingers, and I have to admit their cool, smooth feel is mesmerizing.

"Tangled up?"

"I was hoping *Resurrecting the Dragon* would help me with that. But it disappeared. And according to Louise, there are no other copies left."

Sister G shakes her head and looks at the ceiling. "Well. That's too bad. Though it doesn't surprise me."

"Why?"

"I'm afraid people around here aren't big fans."

"So those people got rid of the book?"

"Could be. I'm afraid some people think out of sight is out of mind. But, of course, things out of sight are still here."

"Now that sounds mysterious," I say. "How can a book that's out of sight still be here?"

"The physical book may be gone, but the story it spoke of will never go away. That's the beauty of a story. It lasts forever."

"Well, I got to look at a few pages, but they were all marked up. I put the book down for a couple minutes and when I came back to it, it was gone. I didn't have time to understand how it would change my life like you said it could." Or why it made me shiver.

Sister G nods. "Marked up. Oh, my." She faces forward again, staring at a gigantic cross on the wall above the organ. An almost naked man, Jesus, according to Mimi, is nailed to it. And he's bleeding. Maybe he was the reason Mimi didn't go to church a lot, even though she was religious like most of the people in town. A crucifixion doesn't exactly fit in with peace. But it doesn't seem to bother Sister G because she just keeps staring.

"Don't you think it's odd that the book—*Poof!*—is gone? How does that happen if nobody else is around except me?"

"It is odd."

"So, what exactly is *Resurrecting the Dragon* about, anyway?"

"I wouldn't want to give away its essence," Sister says, still staring ahead.

"Why not? If stories are supposed to last forever, I'd think you'd want to tell me. Especially if the books have disappeared."

Sister reaches out for the beads, and I hand them to her. She click-clacks them again, moving each one into and out of her hand swiftly. "It's not something that can be explained. You've got to read it and interpret it yourself. That's the only way it can be of help to you, Jett."

"But the book's gone. I can't read it, so why not tell me?"

She rolls a blue bead between two of her fingers for a long time. It's different from the others, not quite a perfect sphere, and made of clay, I think. "Keep trying to find a copy, and if you're still unable, then ask me again."

My face burns with frustration. "Right. I'll keep looking for it. Maybe my x-ray vision can help me out." I feel guilty for being angry with Sister G, but she's confusing me.

Sister G keeps twirling that blue bead and nods.

"Pretty blue, that one. Is it special?"

"My little sister made it for me. I think of her all the time since I use these beads daily." She drops the beads in her pocket.

"You have a sister?" I wonder if little sisters are like little brothers as far as being obnoxious.

"Yes... Well, I did... That is, I do. We just don't see each other much. Today is her birthday."

"Oh. I'm sorry."

"No, it's okay. It's better this way."

Sister G doesn't look like it's okay. She looks like she's trying to make herself believe that, though.

I stand. "You working in the garden today?"

"After my prayers." She folds her hands and bows her head. She's got a lot of prayers in her.

"Want me to start on the watering?"

"Sure. That would be wonderful," Sister G says without looking up. And when she says the word wonderful, it doesn't sound wonderful at all.

"Okay then. I'm on it."

Outside, I fill the watering can and scan the sky for planes. So far, so good. But I need that book, and soon. Besides hopefully curing me, *Resurrecting the Dragon* puts people at a loss for words. Even Sister G. That's some major power, some kind of potent silencing power. Just what I need for the voices in my head. And maybe it'll even work on my brothers.

· · ·

As soon as I get home, I pull Felix from his cage and set him on the bedroom rug. A parasite attacked Felix's nervous system when he was a baby, leaving him blind in one eye, and his head tilts to the right, making him look like a therapist doing some serious listening. But he gets around just fine. Felix makes me smile on days so dark it seems like the sun has lost all its shining power. "Okay, Felix, go run around." He scampers toward the bookshelves. "No chewing, please. Just hopping." And he hops off. I can always count on good old Felix to listen. I pray he doesn't get sick again. Maybe Sister G has herbs she could give him if he does.

I take my matryoshka off the shelf and look into her eyes.

"Mimi, I believe Louise knows more than she's letting on about the missing book. Stealing books is a crime and I doubt Louise would go that far, but you always said to trust my gut, and right now my gut feels suspicious." I turn the doll around and touch the long braid painted down her back. Mimi used to let me braid her hair before she started losing it during her sickness. I'm letting my hair grow long now, just like Mimi's.

I place the doll back on the shelf. "I hope you approve of what I need to do next." Then I sit at my desk with my journal.

TO-DO LIST #135: INVESTIGATIONS
1. Take a peek into Louise's desk drawers. (Just a peek, no rummaging. That would be rude.)
2. Interview people who might know what happened to the book, like _____. (Figure out who those people might be.)
3. Optional: Follow Louise when she leaves the building to see if she does anything suspicious.

(Carry out only if all else fails. She is my friend, after all.)

I tear the page out of my notebook and read it again. My plan is too big for just one person. I'd need an assistant. I fold it and put it in my pocket.

"Come on, Felix, time for supper." I squat to scoop him up, but he bounds away.

"Felix, your fifteen minutes are up. Come back here."

Felix hunkers down under the window where the sun casts a big wedge of warmth. Sometimes my bunny acts more like a cat. He looks so content sunbathing that I hate to disturb him. But I don't have a choice, so I inch over and grab him, holding him close to my chest so his hind legs won't pump too hard and break his back. That's how strong a rabbit's legs are.

"Sorry, buddy, but I have to go."

I feed him a cup of lettuce. Felix's To-Do list is now complete. I latch his cage closed and head for Thellie's. This isn't something that can be discussed by phone.

· · ·

"Yeah, so we've got a major problem here in our little town of Wisteria. Surprising but true."

Thellie plays with the pink yarn flowers on her bedspread and hums a tune from the musical, *West Side Story*.

"You don't think it's just a lost book?" Thellie asks, looking up and squinting at me.

"Thellie. How do you explain the book being there one minute and gone the next? Books can't disappear on their own."

"What's so special about this book that you have to get it back?"

"Well, I liked it. I think. Hard to explain."

"You think? Usually, you have pretty strong opinions."

"I need to read the entire book. It's got the power to change lives."

"Wow. That's a strong endorsement when you haven't even read the whole thing."

"I said it was powerful. I only *heard* that it could change lives."

"Tons of books change lives, I bet. Why not look for another?"

"The fact that Louise said this book has disappeared from every library near here is major. Stealing is against the law. I intend to right the wrong."

"But why would somebody steal all the copies? Even if you love a book, you don't need more than one copy of it."

"Right, and that's why I think someone *doesn't* like the book and wants to be sure *nobody* reads it."

"You mean it's being censored?"

"Exactly. Freedom of speech. Censorship violates the first amendment." I pull my list from my pocket and hand it to Thellie. "You up for helping me carry out my plan?"

Thellie reads it at least twice and hands it back to me. "Sounds sneaky to me."

"Yes, sometimes you have to sneak around to find a sneak, right?"

Thellie sighs. "Look, I'll help you out, but if things get too dicey, I'm out."

"Dicey?"

"Dangerous."

"Right. Of course. There'll be no danger because we won't get caught."

"Thelma! Dinner!" her mom calls.

"I gotta go," she says.

"Meet me at the library tomorrow at eleven-fifteen. Louise gets a break at eleven-thirty on Saturday mornings," I whisper.

"Got it." Thellie bounds down the stairs, and I follow.

"Hi there, Jett," Thellie's mother says. "Stay for dinner?"

I eye the table with three places settings, water glasses at each, and a bouquet of flowers in the middle. Smells of tomato sauce and garlic wander through the room, a tough thing to turn down.

"Thanks, Mrs. Harrison, but I've got to get home to take care of my bunny."

I let myself out, leaving the yummy smells behind for the Harrison family to enjoy—together, at the same table, at the same time they ate dinner last night.

CHAPTER EIGHT

When I arrive at the library on Saturday, I go straight to the reference desk. Louise looks up at me and blinks fast, like she has an eyelash in her eye and is trying to clear it.

"Hello, Jett. How are you today?"

Louise has dark circles under her eyes, and her brown hair, usually worn pulled back, falls free over her shoulders, the ends poking out at different angles like they're rebelling against the change.

"I'm good." I walk closer to her desk. "How about you?"

She looks down and fiddles with a torn page in a book titled, *Know Your Toddler*. She snaps a piece of tape from the dispenser. Her hands shake as she applies it to the rip like a band-aid. Louise sniffs and coughs. "Got a cold coming on, I think. Better keep your distance."

I bite my lip. Is Louise on to me?

"Sister Gia probably could help you with your cold. Her family has used herb tinctures for generations." Hopefully, this kindness will make up for what I'm going to do next.

Louise closes her eyes and shakes her head. "I'll stick with good old-fashion cough medicine, thanks. Tried and true." She flips to another ripped page and stifles another cough with the crook of her arm.

I back up but keep my eyes on her. "Okay. Well, I hope you feel better soon."

I make my way to the middle-grade bookshelves and pretend to look for a book until Thellie arrives. I glance over at the corner, but no Adeline.

At exactly eleven-thirty, Louise leaves her desk with her coffee mug and climbs up the stairs. Thellie passes her on the stairs coming down.

"You're late," I hiss at her.

"Sorry! My mom made me vacuum my room before I came. One of my Saturday chores."

Some kids might say I'm lucky because I don't have Saturday chores. When my mom sees dusty furniture, she asks for help. No warning. I just stop what I'm doing and dust. The lucky kids are the ones with scheduled chores they can count on and plan around.

Thellie follows me to the reference desk, whisper-humming. We fake looking interested in books along the way. When we get there, we scan the area to make sure we are alone.

"Okay, you go to the top of the stairs and hide out," I whisper. "Let me know when Louise comes back."

"This is a library. How am I gonna do that if I can't call out to you?"

"Cough."

"Huh?"

"Clear your throat and cough. That's a normal library sound that nobody will think twice about."

"Got it," Thellie says and goes up the stairs.

I slide behind the desk and kneel.

There are tracks on the rug under Louise's desk where the chair wheels rub. A recycling bin to the side is close to overflowing with papers and old mail. I nudge the chair out of the way and open the bottom drawer. A cup of coins, a pack of computer paper, two boxes of number two pencils. I close that drawer and open the top one. I rise into a squat to see inside. A bible, a clear blue glass paperweight in the shape of a starfish, and a map of the town. (Visitors come into the library a lot to use the bathroom and get directions.) But there is nothing that might be a clue to finding the books or to why Louise looks different today. A not-so-good kind of different.

Checking my watch, I figure I'm safe for another seven minutes. I look around the rest of the area. Portable shelves on wheels, full of returned books. Two empty book carts. A blue lunch cooler on the floor next to them. Chances are slim that it holds a clue, but no stone can be left unturned. I crawl over and unzip the cooler. A sandwich wrapped in wax paper, an apple, and a juice box of lemonade. I zip it up and put it back by the carts.

As I slide past the desk, I notice Louise's computer bag way back underneath. Her bag is personal, like a purse or backpack, and it's extremely bad manners to snoop in someone's personal things. Especially a friend's. On the other hand, I think it might hold a hint about where *Resurrecting the Dragon* disappeared to. Or why poor Louise looks and acts so un-Louise today. Snooping might actually help me help Louise.

I crawl under, unzip the briefcase, and peek in. There's a small book with an emerald green spine. I pull it out. Sure enough, on the cover is a fire-breathing dragon. *Resurrecting the Dragon*. But my excitement deflates fast.

Louise has lied to me.

My hands tremble, but I open the book, and I'm hardly able to turn the pages. A few have been torn out. There are ragged edges, and some marked up pages. On one page just past the middle is a picture of the girl looking inside a cave. On its floor is an odd swirling cloud of blurry images. The caption reads: "The dragon's cave held all the townspeople's memories." The next page shows the girl being confronted by a smoky memory image, a threatening creature, and she's cowering and covering her eyes.

What a shift. She goes from this girl who seems lost in the woods to a scared girl being taunted by a cave creature, but in the end she's brave and uses her fire to turn something to ash. It's hard to understand how she changed since so many pages are missing. Frustrating! Those are the pages I probably need. They must hold the answer to how I can find peace. And to add to the mystery, five blank pages follow the page with THE END on it. Since when isn't the end the end?

My head is buzzing with unanswered questions, but Thellie's coughs interrupt my wonderings. Footsteps click on the staircase, and Louise's legs come into view. I shove the book back into the briefcase, reposition the chair, and sneak away to the middle-grade shelves before she makes it to the bottom. There I apologize to Louise under my breath. If heaven and hell truly exist, I know where I'm headed.

CHAPTER NINE

Outside the library, Thellie and I discuss our next move.

"But why would Louise steal books?" Thellie asks.

"Dunno. Maybe after school on Monday, we can interview some other librarians, see what they know about the missing book. We'll pretend we're getting information about their job as part of a school assignment."

"I'm not into lying."

"It's all in the name of the First Amendment! They're just white lies. They're not gonna hurt anybody."

"Lies are lies, Jett." Thellie walks away.

It looks like I have to carry on alone. It wouldn't harm to make a few phone calls to see if anyone knows where the book might be, or who checked it out. Just to see if Louise's story can be corroborated. It's all in the name of justice.

At lunch on Monday, I fill in Rodney about the disappearance of *Resurrecting the Dragon*.

"Why are you whispering, Jett?" he asks.

I look over both shoulders. "Because the censor could be anyone."

"What's this disappearing book about?" Rodney looks back and forth between me and Thellie.

Thellie shrugs and nibbles a pickle.

"Not sure," I say. "I made a few phone calls hoping to interview some people, but nobody wants to talk about it. That's why it's such a tough case to crack."

"You've seen a copy?" he asks.

"Uh-huh." I pull the wax paper from my sandwich.

"Okay, then what's it about?"

"Lots of pages were missing or marked up. The few pictures I actually could make out were hard to understand without the other pages."

Rod finishes chomping his chips and asks, "What were the pictures of?"

Somebody is finally willing to talk about *Resurrecting the Dragon*. But now I'm not so sure *I* am.

"A lost girl and a cave that holds memories. Some scary ones that she has to battle." I sip my chocolate milk. It tastes rancid. I hold my napkin to my mouth and try to wipe my tongue on it without them noticing, then push the milk carton away.

"Hmmm... That does sound interesting," he says.

"But the book sort of gives me the creeps, too. Like I want to keep reading it, but I also want to put it away."

A headache pinches at the edges of my eyes, ready to make a solid landing.

Shhh!

I shake my head to get rid of the voice, then I shove my food back into my lunch bag.

Thellie raises her eyebrows. "You're not eating much these days, Jett."

"Not hungry."

"You won't have any energy to find that book if you don't eat."

"I'm fine." I hand Thellie my blueberries.

"Maybe that's why the book's missing," Rodney says.

"Blueberries?" Thellie asks incredulously, popping a fistful into her mouth.

Rodney sighs. "No! Maybe the missing book gives other people the creeps, too."

"Could be," I say. "But I have it from a reliable source that the book is worthwhile."

"Who's that?"

"Doesn't matter." I brush some crumbs off the table, and a piece of wax paper falls to the floor with them. I lean down to pick it up.

"Boo!" Lars Dwayne's face beams at me from under the table and I jerk back up, hitting my head on the edge.

"What do you think you're doing?" I ask, rubbing my forehead.

"Just tryin' to see what all the whispering is about." He grins like an evil jack-o'-lantern.

"Mind your own business, Lars," Rodney says. "You okay, Jett?"

"I'm fine."

"Maybe you should make it my business because I can help," Lars tells him, climbing out from under the table. He stands next to me. I step aside.

"My dad is a radio host, and he does tons of interviews all the time. Interviewing is in my blood. You have interview problems? Here I am!" He pumps his fist in the air and makes a muscle with his bicep. Or tries to, at least. "I'm the king of questions!"

"Right. That's questionable," I say, and he puts his hands on his hips. It'd be a snowy day in Hawaii before I'd let Lars help. Too risky to let the son of the notorious Mr. Ed Dwayne in on this. His father chews up anyone who disagrees with him and spits them out like watermelon seeds at a picnic.

"Yeah, well, we'll see, Lars. Right now, I'm in good shape. Thanks anyway," I say.

Lars rolls his eyes and sits back down, glowering at me.

"How dare he eavesdrop on us!" I say to Thellie as she pulls cookies from my bag. "So rude."

Thellie looks at the cookies, then hands them back. She's not a fan of oatmeal.

"Any kind of snooping is rude." Her eyes say more than her words.

Rod looks at us, back and forth. "What is up with you two? It's like you're talking in code."

I scowl at Thellie, then turn to Rod. "Do you believe white lies are okay?"

"Not sure. Lying is lying. It's one of those things where people might not trust you again after you do it."

"*White* lies," I say. "They're different from actual lies. Sometimes you've got to use white lies to get to the truth."

He swallows and slurps some milk. "Not sure about that. Someday, though, they'll invent a robot that can tell if a person's lying just by being in their physical space. No lie detector machines needed."

"You're avoiding the question. Don't you agree that a white lie is okay if it's used to bring justice to the oppressed?"

Rod pushes his chair back from the table. "Whoa. Now you're making this sound like something major, maybe something adults should take care of."

"It is major! But right now, it's the adults who are the problem. Not one of them will tell me anything about the book. If nobody talks about it, then we'll never figure out who's the censor, and this author, S. A. Rahdear, continues to be silenced, denied freedom of speech."

Rodney shakes his head. "Look, if Rahdear really cares about it, they'd speak up on their own, right?"

"I've never heard of the author," I admit. "They could be dead for all I know. But besides standing up for what's right, I want to read that book. I need help to figure some things out."

"Jett, I want to help you, but I'm not sure how. When I create a robot, I've got a detailed plan to follow. Right now, all you've got is a confusing bunch of so-called facts. Let me know when you have a plan, okay?" He picks up his trash. "See you in Social Studies." Thellie waves at me and follows him.

I slump over and put my head on the table. Sometimes it just isn't worth it to argue. I always seem to be on the least popular side of a debate. Might as well keep my mouth shut.

CHAPTER TEN

"I don't know, Sister G, it's like Louise has swapped out being my friend for being a mysterious person with something to hide."

We adjust the sprinklers so the spray reaches the far end of the garden. I pick one up to pull it closer, and it drenches me from the neck up.

"Yikes!" I drop it and the hose flicks around like a confused snake. I kick at it till it rights itself. The spray feels good in the heat, but my hair is sopping.

Sister G laughs and pulls a handkerchief from her sleeve. I dab at my hair as Mr. Ed's voice blares annoyingly in the background. His show comes on right after The Happy Gardener Show that Sister G loves, and by that time she's so busy enjoying her own happy garden that she doesn't even hear Mr. Ed.

But I do. Mr. Ed is in preacher mode again. "You got that right, Jared. Of course, it's a hoax! Their parents put them up to it. Why would a bunch of kids have such strong opinions about gun control? Because their parents do, that's why. Folks, be careful of what you say and do in front of your kids. They're like little sponges, soaking everything up, and it's not always for the good."

"What makes you think Louise has got a secret, Jett?"

I fumble with my thoughts, then make my decision. I clear my throat.

"I found a copy of *Resurrecting the Dragon* in Louise's computer bag after she'd told me there were no copies within at least a fifteen-mile radius of Wisteria. That part she was right about. I asked the librarians at other libraries and none of them wanted to even talk about the book, let alone look for a copy."

Sister G freezes. "Oh, my."

I wither. "Snooping is not something I normally do, I promise. It's just that Louise was acting so mysterious that it felt wrong. I knew she knew more about the book. And I needed to find out what."

All Sister G says is, "Hmm..."

I hand back the hanky. "Louise is my friend, and she's being two-faced. That's not something a friend does."

"No, one wouldn't think so."

Grey Cat sits on his haunches and watches as a mouse scuttles along the garden path past him and disappears into the bushes. The natural order of prey and predator doesn't apply in Sister G's Garden.

"Wouldn't think so? It's dishonest. It's flat out lying," I say.

Sister G puts on her gardening gloves. "Let's not be too quick to judge. One never knows what's going on in a person's life that causes them to behave like they do."

I stare out over the garden. The only sound is the swish-swish-swish of the sprinklers.

Mr. Ed rails on. "... and now a child is rooting around town trying to find out what happened to all the copies of *Resurrecting the Dragon*. This is exactly what I mean, Jared. My show isn't called S.O.S.A.D for nothing! It is *so sad* that any parent who wants to save their child from the consequences of reading inappropriate content must remain extremely vigilant."

I look at Sister G holding a clump of weeds over the bucket, ready to drop them in, frozen in time. Finally, she releases them, turns, and looks at me.

"Oh, dear. What's happening?"

"I'm sorry, I was telling a couple of friends about the book and my talks with the librarians, and Mr. Ed's son heard me."

"I see." Sister G's face is bright red, and it isn't from the sun.

"Why would he say that the book isn't for kids when it's shelved in the middle-grade section?"

She rubs her eyes and stands. "What do you think of a walk to the library? We could use a break. You can show me all your favorite spots."

"Ummm... Okay." She's changing the subject, side-stepping the book, just like everyone else. But she looks so wiped out that I don't push her on it.

We let ourselves out the gate, and as we cross the street to the library, a plane drones overhead. I clap my hands over my ears and close my eyes. My heart whimpers, then races.

Sister G takes my elbow and steers me the rest of the way across the street. "What is it, Jett?"

I scan the sky and exhale. "Nothing. I mean, I don't know. My body clenches up when I hear a plane. Sometimes I have to run inside at recess, and let's just say some kids think it's pretty funny." I cross my arms and poke at a dandelion with my toe. I feel Sister G's eyes on me, and they burn.

"Jet, have you ever been on a plane?"

I shake my head no.

"Did the noise of a plane scare you, maybe when you were younger?"

I swallow the lump in my throat and make my way to the top of the library stairs. "I... I don't know. Can't remember..."

I reach for the door. Sister G takes my hand and leans over to look me in the eye.

"You sound confused, Jett, and that's a sign you might need to talk it out. With your mother, maybe."

"Mom's heard plenty about how I feel about loud noises."

"I'm sure she wouldn't mind hearing more. I'm also willing to listen. There's one thing they train us nuns well for, and that's to be skilled listeners."

My eyes burn. I don't remember the last time I cried. Even when I crashed my new bike, I held it together.

"Jett? You know that, right?"

"Yes. Thanks, but I'm fine." I hold the door open for Sister G. "Come on in. You're going to love the dome paintings."

CHAPTER ELEVEN

"It's due back in two weeks." Louise hands a book to a boy and his mom. When she catches sight of us, she nods at me and gives Sister G a tight smile.

"Sister Gia. It's been quite a while," Louise says.

"Yes, it has," Sister replies.

They look back and forth at each other. A stalemate.

Louise nods and unfolds a corner of a page in *The Wind in the Willows*.

I grumble. "Why can't people just use bookmarks?"

Louise shakes her head.

"It was a travesty that our women's group disbanded," Sister G says. "But I suppose not everyone has time for book clubs."

"Some prefer to avoid heated discussions." Louise clicks away on her keyboard.

Sister G forces her lips into a semi-smile. "To me, that's the fun of book discussions. Hearing everyone's different opinions."

Louise just keeps clicking. Sister G's face goes blank.

"Come on," I say to Sister. "I'll show you something I love."

We take the steep steps to the second floor and gaze up at the wide dome which has seven historical scenes about book-making painted in colorful detail.

"Very impressive, up close like this," Sister says. "And the paintings underneath the scenes... wonderful portraits. All are New England authors."

The curiosity is too much, so I clear my throat and dig in.

"What was all that about a book group with Louise?"

Sister G is wide-eyed, taking in all the paintings. The Wisteria Library dome can do that to a person, no matter how many times you've seen it.

"Louise attended our women's book club at the church a while ago."

"And she quit?"

"Not everyone is cut out for it. Some readers find certain books prickly, and they aren't willing to discuss them."

"Prickly?"

"Yes. Something in the story might make a person feel... well... uncomfortable, or they don't agree with the way an issue is presented. So, they stop reading."

I nod. I can understand that. Sort of.

Sister points at Ralph Waldo Emerson's portrait on the dome.

"Some writing, as you know, makes people very angry. Let's just say that there are people in this town who would crucify Emerson if he were still alive."

My jaw drops. "Crucify?" Images of the man on the cross in the church come to mind.

"Well, perhaps I'm being a tad melodramatic. Let's just say Emerson might not be welcome here."

"Why?"

"Back in those days, his devotion to nature was misinterpreted, I think, by some religious people who accused him of committing idolatry—worshipping someone or something over God."

I look more closely at Emerson's portrait. He doesn't look evil. He looks—

"Whoa! You see that?"

Sister G squints. "What?"

"I swear he winked at me." But it's a dead guy in a painting. Is this book mystery messing up my mind and making me see things that aren't there?

"Trick of light, perhaps," Sister G says. "Or maybe he believes you're a friend."

"Ha. I love nature, too, but I'm no Emerson."

"He certainly had strong opinions and wasn't afraid to voice them. He wasn't fond of institutions or hierarchies like the church."

"Wow. That's super-brave that he spoke up, even when he knew others would get all bent out of shape about it." I cringe thinking about that day with the chess players.

Sister G nods. "Lots to admire in him."

Sunlight spreads over the dome like honey. Mr. Emerson looks especially bright. His stare reminds me of Felix, quiet and curious. Like he's waiting for something.

"Do you agree with Emerson?" I ask. "You love nature, too, but you're still part of the church."

"I think everyone's entitled to their own opinions. But they are not entitled to force them on others. Take your grandmother, for instance. She believed in God, and she prayed, but she didn't attend church regularly. Personally, I would've loved to see her attend the church of her choice, but I respect the decisions she made."

"My parents didn't respect Mimi's choice to pray. Usually, they were all about letting people live the way they wanted, even if it was different from their way. But they didn't want Mimi's religion influencing us kids. They don't want anybody influencing us because they want us to make our own choices. But how do we make a choice if we don't know what the other choices are?"

"You're right about that." She points to the paintings above the authors that circle the dome. "Absolutely breathtaking."

"Louise told me those panels represent the evolution of bookmaking. See the Egyptians gathering papyrus in the first one? And there toward

the end is the Gutenberg press and bible." I look at Sister G. "I guess as a book-maker yourself you know all about it."

"A magnificent interpretation. It shows that bookmaking is something anyone can do if they put their mind to it. Can you imagine the physical labor the ancient Egyptians went through to record their stories? Same with being an author. You need to be tough in many ways." She points at another portrait.

"And there's Harriet Beecher Stowe..." Her voice goes low. "Her book, *Uncle Tom's Cabin*, was so controversial that some people called it garbage."

I scrunch my eyes. "Garbage? Why?"

"Stowe was against slavery and her book depicted it in all its horror. Female slaves, especially, were at the mercy of their male owners."

My scalp sweats and itches even as the air conditioning makes my arms goosebump.

Shhh!

"Go away," I mumble. The voice gets sharper every day.

"What's that?" Sister G asks.

I turn away from Stowe's portrait. "Nothing. The thought of it all is just so horrible."

Sister G circles the floor, taking in all the artwork above us. "Unfortunately, there are still those who believe they are better than other people, and that they have the right to control them. Will we ever learn?"

"Doubt it. Right here in our own town, people rant about what's written in books. And when they don't like a book, they just make it disappear."

Sister G turns away abruptly, shakes her head, and starts down the stairs. Her shoulders slump and her feet drag.

"You okay?" I ask.

"Different interpretations of books are great discussion starters. But when people think theirs is the only correct interpretation and insist that others agree with them, that's a problem. Then others feel intimidated and go silent."

"That's bullying."

"It is. And when it comes to silencing authors, it's censorship."

"Right! Exactly what I'm saying. *Resurrecting the Dragon* is being censored! Why doesn't the author come forward and do something about it?"

At the bottom of the stairs, Sister G stands still. "I'm sure there's a reason the author wants to remain anonymous. The book is already considered by some as inappropriate for children. Maybe she doesn't want to stir up trouble like Stowe's book did."

"She? The author is female?" At last. A clue! "I thought nobody had information about the author."

Sister waves my words away and strides toward the door. "What I'm saying is that whoever wrote it fears something."

"But you called the author she. Do you know who she is?"

Sister G keeps walking. The church bells toll. "Oh, my," she says. "It's later than I thought. I've got to get back and start dinner. Thanks for the library tour, Jett. I'll see you tomorrow." She crosses the road and walks toward the church.

"Wait! You didn't answer my question!" Sister G doesn't even turn around. She just waves her hand in the air. *Resurrecting the Dragon* has done it again. One little book can actually change people's behavior. And not always for the good.

And Sister G... was she quickly becoming another once-trusted person who's suddenly landing on my Friendship Uncertain List?

CHAPTER TWELVE

After Sister G leaves, I take the stairs two at a time back up to the dome. I plant myself right under Ralph Waldo Emerson.

"Pssst! You still there?" I call to him.

The late-day sun is slowly passing by him, leaving his left side in a shadow. "Don't go!" I whisper, thinking maybe it was the sun that brought him to life, then shaking that foolishness out of my head.

I figure I've got nothing to lose. "What do you know about the disappearance of *Resurrecting the Dragon*?"

Mr. Emerson doesn't move a muscle.

"It's a censored book and I need to get it, and you have a bird's-eye view of the library, so I thought you might have seen something."

Not a nod. Not a wink.

"Please?"

Nothing.

"Show me a sign that all my work to get the book back isn't for nothing."

Rats. I rub my neck because it's cramped from looking up so long, then I pick up my backpack and shrug it over my shoulders. As I turn to go, I almost step on a dollar bill.

Wrinkly and worn, it's probably spent time in a bunch of people's pockets. Scrawled in red ink along the edges are seven quotes. Four on the front, three on the back. I'm thinking it must be illegal to mess with money like this. Even without the quotes, the dollar is so old that I can hardly see the eagle on the back. The words, "In God We Trust", are blurred.

It takes a while, but I finally decipher the tiny handwriting. Here's what it says:

"Every burned book enlightens the world."

"Fiction reveals truth that reality obscures."

"Nothing external to you has any power over you."

"What you do speaks so loudly that I cannot hear what you say."

"Adopt the pace of nature: her secret is patience."

"Even in the mud and scum of things, something always, always sings."

"What is a weed? A plant whose virtues have not yet been discovered."

On the back, in the bottom right-hand corner, are the initials: RWE.

I look at Emerson and hold up the dollar bill. "Did you do this?"

No response.

"What should I do with it?"

The sunlight now slants below the portraits. Emerson's completely in the shadows. I squint, then look all around to be sure nobody is witnessing me chatting with a painting.

I tuck the dollar bill in my pocket. As I walk home, thoughts race around my mind like Grey Cat chasing his tail. I've got no idea what to do next.

•   •   •

At home, I stuff the dollar bill in the shoebox with my other lists and have a talk with my matryoshka.

"So many surprising things are happening, Mimi. But one thing's for sure, and that's that I feel better that a guy like Emerson makes lists like me. Check that. Maybe that's a leap. Just because his initials are at the bottom of the dollar bill doesn't mean he wrote those quotes. For all I know, Harriet Beecher Stowe could've written them. I'm sure they'd be fans of each other." I unscrew the matryoshka and remove each nested doll, placing them on my desk. "It's like there's one mystery inside of another, and another, and another."

I take out my journal and go to a new page.

TO DO List #136: IMPORTANT CASE DETAILS TO CONSIDER

1. Talking about *Resurrecting the Dragon* makes everyone quiet or sad. Or angry. Yet Sister G

says the book could help me find peace. Sad and angry don't fit with peace.

2. Some people think the book is bad for kids. What's so bad about a girl exploring a cave or talking to trees? Are there still people around who think communicating with nature is weird or wrong? Is that why the book is missing?

3. Nobody knows or has heard of the author of the book. Maybe they are scared, like Sister G says. But about what?

4. The author appears to be female. I think. How does Sister G know this?

5. Louise has a copy of the book. Is she the censor? If so, where are the other copies?

6. Mr. Ed is against the book, so he could also be a censor. Are there others?

7. Emerson is trying to tell me something with his quotes. Or maybe not. It's too coincidental for the dollar bill list to be there right when I was trying to communicate with him.

Mimi and I had talked about synchronicity a lot. How two things can happen at the right time and place that make them seem connected, but you can't explain why. Like even before Mimi needed help, me and my family had decided to move in with her. That's synchronicity. Perfect timing.

I rip out the page and place the Important Case Details list in my shoebox. My stash of lists is growing so fast that the cover's ready to burst off the box. I secure it with an elastic band and tuck it back onto the closet shelf.

"Was it synchronicity today, Mimi?" I ask my pink matryoshka doll. "Whatever you want to call it, I hope the dollar bill list helps me find that book, because things aren't going too well right now." The pressure behind my eyes these days is more and more excruciating. Those quotes must hold clues.

Mimi told me that the outermost matryoshka doll is painted to look like a grandmother, and the next one is her daughter, and so on through the generations, until you get to the fifth doll, an infant. It's like every woman or girl is part of the one before her, but you don't realize that until you take the grandmother apart. That's where the story begins.

I hold the baby in my palm, not even as big as my thumb. The littlest one holds the stories of all the dolls before her. That's a lot of stories built up over generations, a heavy load for her to carry around, especially since not all stories are happy ones.

"I'm trying to be patient, Mimi, but I guarantee you mom and dad will move us soon, and I've got to find that book before it happens. I don't want to get to the next town and have to start from scratch, looking for peace all over again. Plus, the voices will not shut up. And I'm not ready to leave Sister G."

I put my hand on my belly to calm it. All my confusing thoughts tumble from my head into my stomach these days. If I don't get the book soon, they'll take over my entire body like aliens in a bad sci-fi movie.

Noise from the TV interrupts my thoughts. The voice is annoyingly familiar. Mr. Ed.

"Laura, I believe that if a local author goes against a town's traditional values or insinuates that children should be able to read books about dark topics, he or she should find another town to reside in that is more accepting of their blasphemous ideas. And judging from the spike in my followers on social media, I'd say that most people agree with me."

I sneak out to the living room and listen, out of sight of my mother who's on the couch hemming a prom gown for a neighbor.

"So, Mr. Ed, if I understand you correctly, you believe the author of *Resurrecting the Dragon* lives somewhere in or near our town?"

"First off, the book was donated to all the local libraries. Probably self-published. Second, I'm not certain, but I think S. A. Rahdear is a pen name, which means they don't want to be identified. Both those things point to the possibility that the author is local."

"I've done some research and couldn't come up with any info about S. A. Rahdear, so I suppose you could be right," the interviewer responds.

"People work in mysterious ways, Laura. We all know that dragons have represented the devil since time immemorial. Wisteria is a God-fearing town that certainly does not want to resurrect any dragon. Anyone who doesn't agree needs to leave. It's all for the sake of the children. Why, I have a boy of my own. I'll do whatever I have to do to keep him safe."

I don't realize till I look down that my hands are clenched and my fists are shaking. This guy thinks he's God's number one, right-hand man. How dare he twist things around to suit his own plan!

I burst into the living room. "Mom! How can you even watch this guy?"

My mother drops the dress she's hemming in her lap. "I'm watching a talk show and he happens to be on, that's all."

"Well, change the channel!"

"What's with all this anger?"

"What he is doing is unfair and illegal. It's censorship!"

"He's being dramatic, but it's not like he's confiscating the books from the shelves."

"But someone is! Louise told me there aren't any copies of that book anywhere. And look at all the people who are listening to him and agreeing with him. Since when can't everyone have their own opinion without being silenced by someone who doesn't agree with it?"

"He's worried about his son, Jett. When a parent worries, they sometimes get all fired up and say or do things that might seem a bit over-the-top."

"What's all this noise?" Dad's standing in the doorway, his eyebrows scrunched into a V.

"There's a book I want to read, but I can't because someone stole all the copies. All because Mr. Ed thinks the book doesn't fit in with our town. He calls it dark, and it's not. I don't think so, anyway. I could only read a few pages before that copy disappeared, too."

"You read this book, Jett?" Mom asks, placing the dress on the table.

"Well, not really because someone marked up all the pages."

"And why were you so interested in reading it?" Dad asks.

"Come on, you guys. Think about it. Doesn't it make sense that as soon as people say we should not read a book, you want to read it?"

Mom and Dad looked at each other and shrugged. "She's got a point," Dad says. "And censorship is wrong, no matter which way you look at it."

"Well," Mom continues, "if the book is about something too disturbing, I can understand why adults might want to keep that sort of thing away from their children." She picks up the prom gown and continues sewing. "It's a parent's job to protect their kids."

What about all the kids who go to church and see that cross with a nearly naked guy nailed to it? If that's not disturbing, I don't know what is.

"Mom, first off, the protecting thing might be true for preschoolers, not for kids my age. We're talking about a middle-grade book here. Second, it all depends on how the disturbing stuff is described. Kids go through bad stuff all the time. They need to know they aren't the only ones who feel a certain way."

Mom stops sewing again. "Who feel what way?" She rivets her eyes on me.

"Any way. Especially if it doesn't feel... well... good." I focus on her needle poking out of the peach colored fabric.

"You okay, Jett?" Dad asks.

Shhh!

My heart beats double time and the skin on my back cringes. "I'm fine. I gotta go feed Felix."

"Wait! Jett—"

"What? This is about an author being censored. It's not about me!"

But the way my parents ask so many questions makes me think it *is* about me. Their interrogation makes me want to censor myself and never speak again. Ever.

CHAPTER THIRTEEN

"I'll get the tires," I say, spraying the hose at the rims.

Sister G dries off the windows of the black sedan. I'm helping her get it ready for a funeral the next day. The priest will drive the car in the procession of family and friends attending the cemetery service. I buff up the tire rims with an old rag.

"Looking good, Jett."

"Ouch!" A tiny bulb of blood pops up from a slit on my thumb. "Cut my finger on the metal edge. Who'd think something like washing a car could be dangerous?"

Sister breaks off a leaf from a potted aloe vera plant on the convent steps. She squeezes the aloe juice on my finger, and it stops bleeding and stinging. Magic!

"Sometimes danger lies in small, quiet places. Other times, big, scary places aren't so dangerous after all." Sister G steps back to get an overview of our car-washing skills, then rubs at a smudge on the driver's side mirror.

"Tell me about it," I say. "The other night on the news—before my mom insisted on turning it off so I wouldn't have to watch sad stories—a girl disappeared from a playground. In broad daylight. A playground should be the safest place in the world… Well, that and a library."

Sister G folds the damp towels and motions to me to follow her. She stops to smell the rosebush, then carefully unwinds one thorny vine from another.

"Even a pretty little rose is dangerous," I say.

"The way you're talking today, Jett, I'm surprised you even left your house." Sister G stoops over a pot of geraniums and gently pinches off dead blooms.

Geraniums. My aunt always had two pots of them on their front step. Me and my cousin Anna used to pull off the pink petals, stick them on our nails, and pretend we'd just had a manicure. Back when I lived next door to her. Back when my cousin was still my friend.

"There *were* times when I wouldn't leave the house." I slap my hand to my mouth to push the words back in.

Sister G sits and pats the bench.

I don't sit.

"Want to talk about it?" she asks.

I blink fast, shake my head. "Nope."

"Fear's not our enemy. Just one of our parts that needs comforting, that's all."

I crumple my brow, totally confused.

"Even if something happened a long time ago, the fear lingers and really never goes away," she continues.

"Great. Now *that's* comforting."

Sister G smiles. "Look, all I'm saying is that being afraid doesn't mean you're abnormal or that you need to be fixed. Once you welcome fear into the rest of your family of emotions, you'll feel more peace inside yourself."

"I can see it now. All of us are in the living room. Anger's sitting on the couch watching a gangster movie on TV while his brother, Fear, sits in the corner covering his eyes."

Sarcasm doesn't stop Sister G. "Sometimes talking about the tough things makes them less scary."

Ssssh!

My teeth clench. I can hardly swallow, let alone speak, so I keep the tough words tucked inside my cheek like a squirrel does with acorns. A dragonfly circles us twice and makes a landing on Sister G's knee. She bends down and looks into its eyes.

"When you look at things close up, like this dragonfly here, they can appear a bit sinister." Its eyes are gigantic and practically take up all the space on his head, like an extraterrestrial. "But after a while, when you sit back and just observe it, that's when you appreciate it in all its wonder."

"Is that what's going on with *Resurrecting the Dragon*? People think it's sinister because they're looking at it too hard?"

Sister holds out her index finger, and the dragonfly hops onto it. "Hmmm. Can't be sure. But I believe you understand things better once you step back and look at the big picture."

Okay, enough. I gotta know. "Sister G, I've been trying to understand what's going on with this book for a while now. I think you know something more and you're not telling me."

"Now, what makes you say that?" The dragonfly takes flight, its iridescent wings glittering in the sun.

"The way you act when we talk about the book. I thought you liked it. You say it could be helpful to me, but you won't tell me how. Or you talk in words that confuse me more than they help me understand."

"I'm sorry about that." Sister G sighs, brushes white dandelion fluff off the other end of the bench. She runs a finger along the spaces between the wood slats of the seat as if there's dirt that needs to be brushed away. A hint of a breeze rustles the herbs and roses, and the scent is delicious. I wonder if Sister G's plants are trying to say something to me with their scent, in the same way everything in the garden speaks to Sister G. Do you need a sixth sense to understand nature like Sister and Emerson do? Which reminds me...

"Fiction reveals truth that reality obscures."

"Some pictures in *Resurrecting the Dragon* remind me of this garden." I sweep my arm around as if introducing every one of its inhabitants. The sunflowers nod and bow. "There's magic here, just like there is in the book. You have conversations with plants. Bugs don't bug you. The garden doesn't breathe well when you're not around. What's up with that?"

Sister G looks up at the puffy clouds. "Okay, okay. You're right."

I sit down next to her. "Right about what?"

"I haven't been forthright with you."

"Oh." I'm not sure if this is a good thing or not.

"The truth of the matter is..."

I lean in closer.

"I... I wrote *Resurrecting the Dragon*," she looks at her dusty black shoes.

I screw up my eyes until I see two Sister Gs. "You what? Why didn't you tell me?"

"Remember what I told you about Emerson?"

"Yes. He loved nature and believed in the power of an individual. What's that got to do with the book?" Sister G still looks blurry.

"I could be in big trouble with the church. Remember we talked about freedom to choose? Well, I am not your typical nun. I've made choices that other nuns in my order may not approve of. To say nothing of how those in the congregation might respond."

"What do you mean?"

"Some people interpret the theme of *Resurrecting the Dragon* as putting nature above God."

"That's it?"

"Well, that's part of it."

I stand up fast. "But this makes you as bad as the person who steals your books. You're not standing up for your right to speak!" I remember Mr. Ed on TV, calling for the author to leave town. "And your name is not S. A. Rahdear."

"It's a pen name. The name stands for Sarah. Sarah, my dear sister." Sister G pulls her beads out of her pocket and turns them over until she finds the pretty blue one her sister made. It's hard to think of Sister G as part of a family, but even nuns have to come from somewhere.

She fingers the bead and smiles. "Sarah was a delight, full of joy."

Was? I gulped. Not another death.

"Full of joy... Until she was assaulted."

My mouth drops. My throat closes up like a noose is tightening around it.

"She was eight. Our uncle assaulted her. Sarah was never the same after that. She begged me not to tell anyone. When she turned sixteen, she ran away, and I never saw her again. Now I know that some secrets do need to be spoken."

I cross my arms over my chest, glance around, looking for the best spot to run to in case I throw up. "Assaulted? Like... you know...?"

Sister nods. "Sexual assault."

My brain buzzes even louder now.

Shhh!

The voice snakes through my body down to the soles of my feet. Down to where my words are trapped.

"I'm sorry," I say. "It's..." The smell of decomposing leaves chokes me up. But leaves don't decompose in spring. And there are no leaves on the garden paths, anyway.

"I know," Sister G responds. "It's hard to put into words. That's why I wrote *Resurrecting the Dragon*. It was a way to speak what I didn't speak when I should've. If that makes any sense at all."

Now my head is screaming. The words stagger out of my mouth one by one. "You—you can't blame yourself."

"I do. I prayed and prayed for Sarah after it happened, but she never regained her joy. When she ran away, I still prayed, but nothing changed, even though I believed God heard me. And to show him how deep my belief was, I joined the convent. Plus, I couldn't stand to look at my uncle's face any longer, so the idea of being somewhere else appealed to me." She waves her hand toward the herbs. "This garden restored my sanity and made me realize its healing powers. I couldn't just wait for God to answer my prayers. I knew I had to do something as well. And conversing with nature was the answer I needed."

Feeling dizzy, I plunk down on the bench next to her. "But the book. What does all this have to do with the book?"

Sister G rustles around deep in the pocket of her skirt, pulls out a small notebook, and hands it to me.

On the cover are the words, *Resurrecting the Dragon.* Different from the covers of the other books. It looks like she designed it free-hand instead of having it printed.

I hug it to my chest. Finally! My quiet new life is getting closer. I can feel it reaching toward me like when the snow melts and the first warm day comes, and you know summer is only weeks away. I leaf through the pages. The pictures are in black and white. All the text is hand-written. "This isn't the actual book," I say, holding it out to Sister G.

"It is real. It's the original. A book dummy. I used those pages as a testing ground to make sure things looked right before I spent the time prepping it for the printer. It's a decent replica of the published version."

I open the book and see the girl with the trees, posed just as she was in the published version, minus the color. "She—it's beautiful."

"Her name is Kalice. It's only a simple rendering, but it gets the point across."

I flip the pages. Kalice is asking the trees for directions to the cave. She climbs a mountain and crosses a wide stream to get there. I skip the scary part in the cave. At the very end is the picture of Kalice with her fiery hands. "Why is she—why does she need..." The words lodge in my throat and I cough. My hands shake. I have to put the book down.

Sister G quiets my hands with hers. "Kalice is based on the Hindu goddess Kali. Nobody messes with Kali without life-changing consequences."

I've got lots of questions about Kalice, but I swallow them. They taste sour and sharp, and they scratch my throat.

Shhh!

I grit my teeth. I bite back the voices. Sister lets go of my hands. "Kalice transforms her fear into strength. She does what I wish I'd helped Sarah do by confronting her attacker and breaking the silence."

The bench slats dig into my thighs, and I squirm for a more comfortable position. My knees fight back by bobbing up and down. I try to still them, but my muscles won't listen.

Sister turns my face toward hers.

"The church garden saved me, Jett, just as our family garden was Sarah's safe place. You could see it clearly from the kitchen window. Nobody would touch her there. The plants were her friends. It was the only place where I saw her smile after... after what happened. The garden was where she could be herself again."

Sister G takes out her handkerchief and dabs at her eyes. My own eyes are teary too, and I hold my jaw tight to keep from crying. Grey Cat magically appears looking for supper. He purrs and Sister G reaches down to pet him.

"I wanted to share with others what I learned from this tragedy. It's all about gathering up your power, not just sitting around when something happens, but using your strength to do something about it. You can find that strength in nature, just as Ralph Waldo Emerson believed. Kids need to know that. I find God in nature, and sometimes being in nature is just like praying. It's quiet and relaxing, and you can focus on things better. Yes. Kids need to know that." She stares up at the sky.

I run my hand over the book cover. "But what good is it if kids can't get their hands on this book?"

"It *was* good for a while... until pages were defaced and torn out, and the books disappeared."

"What was on those pages that bothered people so much?"

"Turn to the middle of the book." I do. "In the story, Kalice must come to terms with her dragons or the memories of things that stand in the way of her making peace with her trauma. Along the way, nature shows her how everything connects and changes, and if you can just be patient with the process, you'll come away stronger. The process isn't always pretty, but it ends well if you allow it."

"And why would a good story like that offend Mr. Ed and his people?" I despise Mr. Ed so much right now that I grip the book so tight it trembles.

"The topic of abuse isn't one you see much in children's books. Some adults don't think it's appropriate. Between that and the fact that Kalice prays to trees and gets advice from nature, *Resurrecting the Dragon* is not a fit for a town like Wisteria."

Sister's words, along with all the scents floating around, make me even woozier, and I struggle to steady myself. I want to run away, but if I stand, I know I'll fall.

"Flip to the back of the book," Sister G says.

I do it. There are five blank pages after the page that says THE END, just like the copy in the library.

"Shouldn't THE END be on the very last page?"

"Instead of Sarah's book having an ending, I wanted it to actually be the beginning for others who were abused to tell their stories. Many readers wrote their own stories on the blank pages, and when there weren't any left in one particular copy at Wisteria Library, a girl taped pages with her story into the back cover."

"That's a lot of girls with stories. All inside one book."

Sister G nods.

"So, *Resurrecting the Dragon* got kids to speak up... until they were shut down."

Sister G rolls the blue bead between her fingers. "Every girl's story was like another bead on a special necklace. And it was beautiful. Until it all disappeared. I'm afraid tough decisions are ahead for me."

I jump off the bench. "What? Wait. You're not gonna listen to stupid Mr. Ed and leave town."

"It all depends. Right now, I'm not feeling much love here."

My eyes burn with sadness. Or maybe it's anger. "This book was your way of getting Sarah's voice out there, and now someone has silenced it again."

"You're right." Sister tilts her head and rubs her neck.

"Okay. Then what about the power you told me all girls have? What about getting up and doing something instead of sitting around waiting for something to happen?"

What you do speaks so loudly that I cannot hear what you say.

Sister G stands, leans against the trellis, and breathes in deep. "It's been a long road. I'll let the fragrances of the roses and herbs work their magic. They often have a way with fear. And with sadness."

"But that's just like waiting around for prayers to work. You took action and wrote the book for a reason. You can't just let it all go now."

"Right now, I'm stuck in a town that won't even consider my actions without judging them first. *Resurrecting the Dragon* has no life here."

"But it could come back to life if we fight for it!"

She shakes her head. "The resistance to the book is so high that even if there were one or two people who would stand up for it with us, it wouldn't be enough. Maybe in some other town..."

This is hard. The energetic, upbeat nun I knew is wilting right in front of my eyes. Unfortunately, people aren't like my brothers' comic book superheroes. They can't deflect bullets with a cape or fly away when a villain comes around. Humans have to use their minds when a challenge comes up.

I stand next to Sister G so close that our arms touch and I link mine through hers. "Please. Don't leave town. I promise to help you."

Yikes. Once again, in the garden, my words come out uncontrolled. What if I don't do any better with this promise than I am doing with my promise to Mimi?

Sister G smiles. "Thank you, Jett." She puts her other hand in her pocket and clicks her beads. "I'll see you tomorrow. Right now, I need to go inside and dice potatoes for Sister Patrice. She's still under the weather."

"Wait." I hold the book out to her. "You forgot this."

"You keep it for now. See if it speaks to you." She shuffles away.

I ruffle the pages, wondering how things might change now that I have the book and can look at it closely. Even though it isn't the published version, it's the original, maybe even more special because of that. It's where everything began. Like the grandmother matryoshka doll opening up and releasing all the dolls inside her. This is the first place where Sister G's thoughts landed and then took off, all in the name of Sarah.

Nothing external to you has any power over you.

Resurrecting the Dragon is powerful, that's for sure. But no book has power over a person's mind. The reader has to decide if its words are true or important. They decide for themselves only, nobody else.

I slip the book into my back pocket. I decide there's no way I'll let Sister G disappear like her books.

CHAPTER FOURTEEN

"Listen, you guys, I've got to find out who's stealing the books. It's now officially urgent."

Rodney scrunches up his nose and cocks his head. "What books?"

I look at Thellie for support. Thellie looks at her feet and hums a song that I vaguely remember from *Mary Poppins*. Mrs. Markat glares at all of us. Her eyes say that study hall is a time to study, not chat. Thellie quits her humming.

"The books I told you about that disappeared from the library," I whisper-yell.

"And remind me why they're special?" he asks.

"Ugh. They've been stolen! I've told you a thousand times. Not only a book, but an author's voice has been stolen."

Rod and Thellie look at me like I'm the suspicious one.

"There's got to be more to it if people want the book off the shelves," Rod says. Thellie nods. "But pay no mind, you'll tell us when you're ready."

I put my hand on my back pocket and feel the heat, the power of Sister G's book, urging me on. When I got home yesterday, I read it cover to cover. Then I read it again. The first time, I wasn't sure what to make of it. The second time, Kalice spoke to me in a way that confused me, even scared me. I put the book down at least three times. Walked away from it. But it called me back mysteriously, like when you have a toothache, and your tongue keeps going back to that tooth even though you know it'll hurt when you do it. Sister G created Kalice, and I was determined to stick up for her. For both of them.

"Guys, it's a matter of what's right and just."

"Sounds like you've been studying for a history test," Rodney says.

"I didn't learn right and wrong from a book. I know it in my heart. And I need your help."

"This means a lot to you. Like you're taking on a crusade," he says.

I nod. "Yeah. It does." I stare at a book on the shelf titled, *A Teen's Guide to Friendship*. That book should be double the size it is. Friendships can be mystifying.

Rod and Thellie's eyes lock on me, expectant. "Okay, listen," I say. "You know how Mr. Ed rants about the book and its dark topic?" They nod. "The topic *is* terrible. But it's also hopeful." I pause and make a decision. "I was told it's about a girl who was assaulted, but through nature she finds the courage to speak up and confront the guy."

There. I said it.

Silence.

Surprisingly, Thellie is the first to speak. "I'm in." She sits up taller and throws back her shoulders. "One of my cousins was assaulted at college. She's in therapy and it helps a lot, but it's been really hard for her."

Rodney looks at Thellie with soft eyes. "I'm sorry about that." Then he looks at me. Differently. Like he was seeing me as a different person.

"I'm in, too," he says. "Nobody should have to go through that."

Tears start, and I manage to hold most back, but not before Rod notices. He puts his hand on my arm and I look away, but don't push it off.

I get it together. I've got a job to do. "Okay, Rodney, can you feel out Lars and see if his dad has mentioned anything about who he thinks might be stealing the books?"

"Absolutely."

"Thanks. And Thellie, I'm planning to call into Mr. Ed's radio show this weekend. I'll definitely need moral support, and somebody I can practice what I'm going to say with so I can be totally prepared. You in?"

"Yes," she replies, though she starts to hum *Follow the Yellow Brick Road*.

"Great! We're fighting to uphold the first amendment of the Constitution of the United States." I can practically hear the Star-Spangled Banner in the background, but what's most clear is the image of Sister G and her sister, the victims of all this nonsense.

The bell rings. Rodney gathers up his things. "If you need anything, I'm here," he says.

"Call me when you're ready to practice," Thellie says, and walks down the hall to her locker. She winds her way around some older kids sitting on the floor talking, bookbags strewn all around, nearly tripping over a boy's leg as she tries to get to her locker. He doesn't move an inch. His eyes are riveted on the guy across from him, telling a story with his hands.

Lightbulb! A little thing known as body language. It's loud without speaking a word.

Maybe making a call to Mr. Ed on the SOSAD show isn't loud enough. Maybe I need to do something big, something more dramatic.

I can't wait till school's over to tell my friends about my revised plan.

•   •   •

"That's right, a sit-in, like back in our grandparents' day. It's a respectable form of activism. Like tree-sitting or protest marches. Peaceful but powerful. We'll need signs, and I'll need a megaphone to lead the chants."

Thellie's eyes bug. "Chants? No way."

"I don't love the idea either, but people walking by the radio station need to know why we're sitting on the steps. Our mission needs to be clear if we want their support."

"I'd like to know more about what I'll be chanting about," Rodney says. Thellie nods.

"Censorship, of course."

"Jett, you can't expect us to follow you blindly without knowing all the little details," he argues.

"Like I told you in the library. People are censoring a book because they don't agree with it for moral or religious reasons."

Thellie gulps. "My parents probably won't go for it. We go to church, you know."

"My Mimi was probably as religious as your parents, but I know she'd agree that when a person is bullied, the right thing to do is to speak up. Doesn't matter if we have the same opinions as the person or not. Anyway, wouldn't God want us to help someone in need?"

Thellie's face goes blank. Right now, I'm not even sure there is a God, and I bet it's going to be a while before I figure it all out, but I'm trying to argue in a way that Thellie can relate to.

"Look, I'm gonna be late to feed Felix if I don't hurry up. Don't worry about it, Thellie. Do what you need to do."

Rodney stands strong as the sun beats down on us. "Censorship. Bad idea, Wisteria. I bet I could figure out some catchy chants."

"Thanks, Rod! Thell, would you maybe be willing to do behind-the-scenes work?"

"Like…?"

"We need signs. And stuff to hand out like pamphlets or bookmarks. And we need other kids to sit-in with us."

"I'll think about it."

Rodney scratches his head. "Considering we'll be advocating for every voice to be heard, especially those who aren't mainstream, maybe we should wear something outrageous. Let me brainstorm that, too."

"Great!" I slap him on the back. He blushes.

"I could probably make bookmarks with nature designs?"

"Thanks, Thellie, you're the best."

Sometimes it's tough to tell if a person truly believes in something or if they're just following along because they don't want to be different. But I don't care. I need all the help I can get.

CHAPTER FIFTEEN

TO-DO LIST #137: RADIO STATION SIT-IN

1. Find outrageous outfits—Rodney
2. Practice what to say—Me
3. Spread the word to meet on the radio station steps at 10 am Saturday—All of us
4. "Borrow" megaphone from gym teacher and return it before first period on Monday—Me?
5. Make *Resurrecting the Dragon* bookmarks to hand out—Thellie
6. Make signs and pamphlets—All of us
7. Do Mimi's breathing exercises to stay relaxed and strong—Me. Over and over again.

At Goodwill, Rodney finds tee-shirts with the Save The Children logo on them. It's a stretch, but it works. Saving the book might save some children. He also finds cool pink caps with dinosaurs on them that say, "Gone but not forgotten!" Again, a loose connection to the disappearance of *Resurrecting the Dragon*. Rod does look pretty good in pink, though.

Saturday is overcast and gloomy, but my new pink cap perks me up.

"Where are you off to so early?" Mom asks.

"I'm meeting some friends at the library to work on our social studies project." It's a stretch but certainly not a full lie. What we're doing fits right into our social studies curriculum. Not exactly the truth, though, either. My secrets are building up, but telling the whole truth comes with its own set of troubles.

We huddle under the Town Hall's overhang, and being the end of May, it's not too cold. A few kids in our social studies class agreed to come, and they're holding signs saying, "Sit-in Against Silencers." Rod got some of his friends from Robotics Club to join in by asking them to bring the robots they created and to program them to hand out flyers. They're sure to draw attention, and it's a perfect way for those kids to test out how well their robots perform.

A lot more people show up than I expect, especially with the rain and all. But it's a Saturday and everyone's out running errands. People are curious and they stop to see what we're up to.

"Stop the silencers!" I yell into the megaphone that I swiped from Mr. Jarret's office. The idea of explaining to him why I needed it made my teeth clench. So, I figured that if I cleaned it up well before returning it in secret, it wouldn't be such a bad thing.

More in the white lie category than an outright wrong.

"Stop the silencers!" I yell again, looking at Rodney and the others to echo me. They do, but it's not the resounding response I'm hoping for.

A woman walking her poodle smiles at us and exclaims, "Aren't you children smart! Courageous, too. Who is this silencer you're talking about?"

I hand her one of Thellie's bookmarks with *Resurrecting the Dragon* on it. The woman's smile melts away.

"Oh. Oh, my. Not for children. Be careful." And she walks away, her poodle prancing along behind her. But she's just one person. There's a whole crowd left to convince.

More and more people gather by the minute. The robots are killing it, approaching men, women, and kids with the freebies. Some people accept the bookmarks, but a bunch of others hand them back once they see what's on them. Talk about crowd mentality; intelligent people would at least ask a question or start a conversation. Just another example of how Wisteria stifles.

But two girls are totally into one of the robots, chatting with it as if it were human, patting it on the head and laughing. They take a handful of bookmarks and start passing them out to others. As if they can feel my stare, they look over at me and wave.

What? The chess girls from the library? Maybe Amelia and Kit don't realize I'm the same person who tried to get them to be quieter that day in the library. I don't look like that person anymore. That person didn't have much to say. They give me the thumbs up and keep mingling with the crowd. Makes sense, I guess, those girls standing up for free speech.

I take a deep breath. "Hopefully, the censor will show up. I'd like to see who it is," I whisper to Rodney. "Maybe there's more than one of them."

Rodney nods and heads over to troubleshoot a robot glitch. Jerry's transmitter must be on the blink. The robot is stuck in one place, its arm extending and retracting over and over. Right next to him stands Louise. I look away fast and begin another chant. A couple of kids from school echo the chant, but lots of adults shake their heads. Some even laugh. Next thing I know, a van from News Channel 8 pulls up and a woman and cameraman get out.

"Jett." Louise is beside me. She holds out her hand. In it is my bunny earring that I hadn't even realized I'd lost.

"Thanks," I say, and take it from her. "Where was it?"

"Under my desk." Now she's glaring at me. "What were you doing snooping around in my things?"

"I—nothing—I was only…"

"What's your name, miss?" The Channel 8 reporter pushes Louise to the side and puts her microphone under my chin.

I turn away from Louise and toward the reporter. "Jett. Jett Jamison."

"I'm Carol Keene. Can you tell us a bit about what's going on here?"

"Well—"

Suddenly, all eyes focus on something behind us.

"I'll tell you what's going on. Heresy, that's what!" Mr. Ed makes his way through the kids sitting on the steps, stumbling over someone's sign. He stands in front of us with his hands on his hips. Lars joins him.

"That book is the devil incarnate! It is not a book for children. Let kids be kids. Leave the adult subjects to the adults." He puts his arm around Lars's shoulders. Mr. Ed's lip trembles. Was he sad? Or just mad?

Some people in the crowd start to clap. Lars looks up at his father as if he were a king.

"You have no right to keep any book away from anyone, kids included!" I shout. "It's our right to read it, and it's the author's right to write it. It's called freedom of speech."

"The book is inappropriate for children," Mr. Ed yells back. "This author has gone against the very soul of this town, and it's divisive. Children shouldn't be discussing such personal stories, especially disturbing ones."

Lots of people cheer. Others just watch.

"Not everyone agrees with you," I say. "Everyone deserves the right to form their own opinion. After reading the book, that is."

Louise's face has softened, but she's chewing her lip.

I'd let Louise down, and I refuse to let another friend down. I must keep my promise to Sister G and make some of these folks understand.

The reporter continues. "If you've never read the book, Jett, then why do you want to save it?"

"Well," I hedge, "I actually did read a few pages of it in the library, but then someone stole it." I scowl at Louise. "Anyway, it's not just the book I want to save. It's the author."

"But the author is unknown, right? How can you save someone unknown?"

"To be honest, I do know the author." A few people gasp. Including Rodney.

Mr. Ed steps up to the reporter. "That's hogwash! That book has been around for several years. Nobody knows the author. How could you know the author? If we knew who the author was, they'd be paying the consequences." And he walks away, shaking his head.

I shout at his back, "Let's just say that the author is someone a lot of you know, and you should help her out by standing up for her."

Louise and I exchange glances. She fingers the cross around her neck.

"So, it's a woman!" the reporter says. "Well, I'll be..."

The rain's really coming down now, and I'm thankful for our pink caps. Louise stares, burning a hole in my cheek. I turn to her and whisper, "You know who it is, don't you?"

Louise nods as she tugs even harder on her necklace, making red lines on either side of her pale neck.

"Then why—" I couldn't stand her disrespect for one second longer. "Then why won't you speak up and support her?" Louise shakes her head and walks away.

"You should support her!" I yell. "Sister Gia is our friend!"

I clap my hand over my mouth. The crowd murmurs.

Rain drips down the sides of Carol Keene's face as she tries to get situated under the camera man's umbrella. Mr. Ed steps toward the microphone.

"A nun, is it? In our very own community? Writing a children's book with an adult theme and, beyond that, defying the church by saying that nature is the healing spirit we need to revere? That's blasphemy! She's a witch! Only witches pray to nature, and witches do not belong in our town!"

Several people begin to chant, "Get her out! Get her out!" Others take the *Resurrecting the Dragon* bookmarks and poke them onto the pointy tips of their umbrellas, swooshing them around like swords and chanting, "Slay the dragon! Slay the dragon!"

I'm facing a beast. I need a dragon for protection. Sister G would need one even more, now that I'd blown her cover.

"This is all so barbaric, so Middle Ages, so pre-twentieth century," I say to Rodney. "I should've known. Nothing good ever comes from loud voices."

Rod pulls his cap down over his eyes and shivers. "Now what?" he asks.

CHAPTER SIXTEEN

Keeping the peace is the toughest promise I've ever made, and once again my shame about disappointing Mimi hangs over me like fog on a beach. Instead of a peaceful sit-in, I've inspired a riot. I know from Social Studies lessons that witch hunts happened all over New England, including Wisteria. Maybe this town has never outgrown it. Wisteria still wants to persecute, to strangle voices like its namesake weed strangles other plants.

I run toward the church. The rain has let up and steam rises from the warm sidewalks. Outside the convent, a mob of people chant, demanding to see Sister G. I stand on tiptoe, trying to get a glimpse of anyone inside, but curtains cover the windows. The protesters are so loud that I fear the healing garden will wither. After all, it's used to peace and respect.

"Jett."

Louise reaches for my arm and draws me aside. I gulp and prepare myself for the blame I deserve.

"Jett, I understand what you were trying to do. I may not agree with how you went about it, but I know your intentions were true."

"But why did you steal the book? Why did you lie to me about what happened to it?" I ask.

Louise closes her eyes. "First of all, I wanted to save the last known copy of the book. There's a lot of pressure from the town to uphold the majority's views. They were against the book, and they wanted it removed. If the town doesn't like what goes on at the library, they can withhold funding. We get personal donations, but it's the town funding that keeps our doors open. I wasn't about to burn the book, for goodness sake, I wanted to protect it until I could figure out what to do. There was danger in leaving it on the shelf."

"Where did you put all the books, then? I know there's more than one of them."

Louise shakes her head. "The book in my briefcase is the only one I have. When I realized the others had disappeared from the shelves at Wisteria as well as other libraries, I knew it was my duty to save the last one. I've no idea where the others are." Her eyes had lost the sparkle that used to make her Louise.

"But do you believe the book is blasphemy like Mr. Ed says?"

Louise pulls at the cross on her necklace. "I'm not sure, Jett. I need to read it again to see how I feel. But even if I don't like what the book says, it doesn't mean the author should be driven out of town or that people shouldn't read it."

Phew. My friend Louise was back. Or maybe she never left. I jumped to conclusions without giving her a chance to speak. "Thank you, Louise. How about we work together? How about you and me and the other librarians get together—"

A whoosh thunders through the air. The crowd screams. One man lunges at a guy holding a torch over a pile of papers. At the corner of the building, orange and red flames surge higher and higher toward a window on the first floor. The air stinks and grey ashes flit around like dirty snow. I glance at the garden, hoping that if Grey Cat's in there, he's hunkered down safely behind a bush.

Within seconds, it seems, fire engines and police cars arrive on the scene. Fifteen minutes later, the fire is out, and the crowd slowly breaks up.

Louise has not left my side.

"This is creepy," I say. "Everything feels so out of control."

Louise takes my arm, and we approach the building. In the ashes are remnants of the bookmarks and flyers we'd handed out, along with my pink cap that I must have lost running to the church. The rim of the cap is tinged black, and the dinosaurs are a blur. I pick it up and put it on anyway. Soot clings to the side of the building, reaching to just below the window which, luckily, wasn't open. If the curtains had caught on fire, the whole convent could've gone up in flames. These people weren't fooling around. All because of a little book. I put my hand on my back pocket to assure myself that *Resurrecting the Dragon* is still there.

"Can I give you a ride home, Jett?"

"No. No thank you, Louise. I'd like to walk." I shuffle my foot in the dirt. "And Louise, I am so sorry that I snooped in your desk and bag. It was rude and wrong and not something a friend would do."

Louise puts her arm over my shoulder. "Sometimes we get something important in our head and we see nothing else but that one thing. I'm guilty of that too. So, I also apologize for not being completely honest with you."

We hug, and Louise goes to her car.

A light flicks on in the convent, so I knock on the door. After a few minutes, I knock again. "Hello? Anybody home?"

Sister Patrice opens the door, looks me up and down, and bites her lower lip. "Yes, Jett. What can I do for you?" Her voice sounds stronger. Maybe the herbs have worked after all.

"Hello. Would you tell Sister G that I'm here?"

Sister Patrice brushes down the front of her skirt. "Sister Gia is not here."

"Okay, then when she gets back, would you tell her I'll come by tomorrow?"

"She won't be here."

"Why? How do you know?"

"She's gone for good. Her closet is empty. She left no note."

Heat flushes my body from my face down to my toes. She hadn't been driven out of town by the crowd. She'd been driven out by me. Gone, just like with Mimi, and I could've prevented it.

Sister Patrice shakes her head and pushes the door closed. I stare at the doorknob until my tears morph it into a blurry blob. Then I walk over to the garden. Usually, I can feel the garden inhale through the slats of the fence and exhale through the gate, but today it's as if it were holding its breath, the plants suspended in time, minus their sparkle, just waiting until their friend and protector return. The roses slump away from the trellis, and the vegetables have begun to shrivel. But there'd be no more pruning or weeding or watering. No more Sister G.

CHAPTER SEVENTEEN

When I get home, the TV is blaring. My parents and brothers crowd around the news.

"There's Jett!" Bo points at the screen. "She's famous!"

I slip past the living room, and just when I think I'm free and clear, Dad calls me.

"Jett, that was one heck of a social studies project."

I gulp. Here it comes.

"And we support you standing up for the nun."

I walk back to the living room. "I thought you didn't like organized religion."

"I'm not so sure this is only about organized religion." He exchanges glances with Mom. "From what I can tell, it's about censorship. And I don't condone censorship no matter who is being censored. I applaud what you tried to do."

"Yeah, but instead of me making a point about the book, I gave away Sister G—um, the nun's—identity, and now...now she's left town." I can't hold it in any longer. Crying always feels like it won't end, a downpour, and now here it is happening just like that. "Why do the people I care about always leave? Either that, or we leave them."

Mom takes my hand and hands me a tissue. "And how do you know this nun?"

"She works in the garden across from the library. But now, who knows what she'll do?"

"I know the garden," Dad says. "A colleague is working on plans to renovate the convent. Says the nuns always want to feed him when he's there. A nice bunch."

"And now the nicest one is gone," I say.

"You were trying to honor her as an author, and your tongue slipped, that's all."

"Because I needed a better plan. I should've written out a speech before the sit-in just in case a reporter asked me questions. I made a sit-in to-do list, but it wasn't good enough."

"You're too tough on yourself, Jett," Dad says. "And if you'd told us all that was going on, maybe we could've helped somehow."

"I didn't think you'd want to help. Anyway, my friends helped, but I was the one who came up with the plan. And it just wasn't good enough."

Mom squeezes my hand. "You did your best, Jett. That's all you can ask of yourself."

"I've gotta clean Felix's cage." She nods and turns off the TV.

In my bedroom, I gather up Felix in my arms and kiss his soft, furry head. "You still love me, right, little guy?" I rub him between his ears. "Please don't leave me. I will be extra special attentive to your needs so you don't ever feel like you want to live somewhere else."

Which reminds me. I need to check my to-do list about caring for Felix. With all that's going on, I'm sure I've forgotten something. I put him back in his cage and pull the shoebox off the closet shelf. When I slip off the elastic, the top pops off and some of the lists fly out and onto the floor.

"No-good, stupid lists. Why am I even checking Felix's? Lists and plans are worthless."

I pick a list from the box and, without even reading it, throw it onto the floor and nail it with my foot, squishing it into the rug. It feels good. Then, I take a handful of lists, then another, my hand on auto-pilot, tossing them to the floor, a pile of papers that have outlived their purpose. I kick them, sending them into a flurry all around the room.

"I can't stand this anymore!" I yell as loud as I can, hoping my words go as far as Wisteria Library and beyond. "I hate this world! It's not fair!"

My body's on fire and my nails bite into my palms. I lean over and gather up a bunch of lists and tear them into a zillion pieces. Then I throw them back down and gather up some more. I tear at them with more force than is necessary, feeling my strength, easy and certain. When every single list is destroyed, my bedroom carpet looks like it's covered in a blanket of white feathers.

And that's when I remember Felix.

"Oh my gosh, Felix, I'm so sorry!" He's huddled in the corner of his cage. I scoop him up and hold him tight. "Just when I promised I'd take extra special care of you, I scare the heck out of you."

I sit on the floor with Felix in my lap and cry some more, tears dripping onto Felix's black back.

When they let up a bit, I look over at Mimi's matryoshkas.

"Now what, Mimi?" I ask. "I've inherited all your stories, but don't know what to do with them. Maybe they're too heavy for me to carry. Maybe you shouldn't have trusted me with them in the first place."

One doll seems to wiggle back and forth like when Mimi shook her index finger at me or my brothers, warning us to think differently.

"I remember, Mimi. You told me that if I kept being pessimistic, peace would never come. Peace is something organic that grows from seeds that only I can plant and tend myself. I remember."

Felix hops onto the floor and sniffs around the wreckage. Before I know it, he's inside the empty shoebox, and the only visible things are his pointy black ears. Sweet, playful Felix.

Even in the mud and scum of things, something always, always sings.

Emerson. A Forever Optimist. Like Mimi.

But if something is singing now other than my dear bunny, I don't hear it. So, I listen harder.

Scritch-scratch. Scritch-scratch.

"Felix, what are you digging at?"

I crawl over to him. He stops digging and looks up at me.

"Whoa! Will you look at that?" Felix is sitting on the dollar bill list that's all crumpled into a corner. It survived my tantrum. How I missed it, I don't know.

I slide the list out from under Felix. Luckily, the only damage done is a small tear in the upper left corner. The quotes are still readable. I read through Emerson's list again. One quote stops me cold.

Adopt the pace of nature: her secret is patience.

Right then, I know exactly what my next step has to be.

"Felix, you are a genius."

Surprise, surprise. I hadn't even needed a to-do list.

CHAPTER EIGHTEEN

I gather up the shredded lists and put them back into the shoe box. Even in pieces, I need to keep them. They represent almost a year of planning step stones for peace. But now that I have a copy of *Resurrecting the Dragon*, my life should be totally peaceful, right?

Wrong. Right now, life couldn't be much worse. But I have a new plan, thanks to Emerson. Maybe I can make life just a little bit better.

I get into bed with my clothes on and pretend to be asleep. When I finally hear Dad turn the big lock on the front door and come upstairs, I wait five minutes, then sneak downstairs and slip outside into the night.

I walk the familiar route quickly. Things look so different in the dark. Tree branches are like arms reaching out, and every so often the flapping of a flag in the breeze sounds like somebody's heaving breaths after a long run. I unlatch the convent garden gate, closing it slowly to keep the creak quiet. I crouch down and make my way along the fence to the bench by the pine tree, just past the roses.

In daylight, the sun washes Sister's garden all bright and hopeful, but tonight it's one big blanket of bleakness. Grey drips from every leaf and branch, a gloomy mist. The heat hasn't let up, and I tug at the wet neck of my tee-shirt as I look around.

"Grey Cat, where are you?" I whisper.

I am in Sister G's garden without Sister G, and it feels off, like wearing someone else's shoes. Being patient in the dark isn't easy. One streetlight provides just enough light to create creepy shadows.

"Psst! Grey Cat, you here?"

I get down on my hands and knees and crawl along the edge of the garden, peeking into all the plantings with my phone flashlight. Grey Cat is nowhere. When I get about a quarter of the way around the garden, I come to an empty bowl on the pathway. Someone had the sense to put water out for Grey Cat but hasn't kept it filled. I take the bowl, crawl over to the faucet, and fill it up. I put the bowl back by the path and keep my eyes peeled. If anywhere, he'd be under one of the four benches since that's where I'd seen Sister G feed him food scraps and, on special days, catnip that she grew in pots. Not being a mouse-chaser, Grey Cat relied on Sister for food.

The weather is on my side. It's so hot that it's not long before Grey Cat slinks between the slats of the garden fence and makes his way to the water bowl. I scramble over to him, stroke his warm fur, and nuzzle his neck as he drinks.

"Grey Cat, I'm so glad you're still around, and I hope you haven't been hungry."

Grey Cat flops down and exposes his white underbelly. I give him a good rub and then take out a baggie of cornflakes and sprinkle them on the grass. He scurries over and eats. As he does, I fold my note to Sister G around Grey Cat's collar as tightly as I can, then tie it in place with a shoelace. I know Sister G will be back. Grey Cat relies on her too much. Now all I can do is go home and wait patiently.

I pull a few weeds as I walk toward the gate.

What is a weed? A plant whose virtues have not yet been discovered.

I hold the weeds to my nose and sniff. "Not a bad smell once you get used to it. Nothing wrong with these weeds, really. Except they aren't always nice to flowers."

I sit on the bench and scan the garden. It misses Sister G. The roses need dead-heading, and their faded petals make the daisies next to them look weak, begging to be saved. A domino effect. One thing goes bad, then another and another until it's all out of control.

I hold the weeds to my nose again and pull them quickly away. This time they smell like pine. Ick. "I don't know, Mr. Emerson. Does every weed really have a virtue to be discovered?"

I sniff again. Deep.

Pine. Autumn. My stomach clenches and I drop the weeds and kick them under the bench. Time to go.

But in the corner of the garden, the spruce tree catches my eye. Its needles have turned brown and are starting to shed. Maybe it's giving up, too. I think about the pictures in *Resurrecting the Dragon*, how Kalice went from sad to hopeful when she spoke to the tree. Nature helps humans as much as humans help nature. A symbiotic relationship. We'd learned about it in science. Living things rely on each other.

Reluctantly, I hold my breath, walk over to the tree, and give a branch a pat. The needles pinch. Yucky old pine. The last few years, we'd had a fake Christmas tree because the smell of a real one made me throw up.

But I put my arm around the trunk anyway and rest my head on the branches. "Life is so unpredictable. Just when things seem good, something happens, and life gets shaken up so bad it shivers like a snow globe scene."

The spruce drops a baby pinecone by my foot.

I smile and pick it up. "Thanks." I look up at the tree's tip-top branches, the place where somebody might place a star at Christmas time. At that very moment, stars begin to pop out of the black sky, one by one, like a choreographed light show. One flashes on and off like a beacon.

But it isn't a beacon.

And it isn't a star.

It's a plane. And it drones louder and spookier than any other.

I gasp, shield my eyes, and drop to the ground with a thud. I cover my ears, but the noise comes so sharp and deep that it cancels out any other sounds around me. I'm on my side, curled into a ball, but I keep looking up. I have to.

Dry autumn leaves crinkle under me. The moist ground seeps through my shorts and my shirt. I see the tops of a zillion pine trees. I never lose focus of the plane way above them.

If I do, I'll die.

It isn't happening. It just isn't. As long as I watch the plane, what's happening to me isn't real. So, I follow it creeping slowly across the sky, hardly making headway, until finally, it disappears. Bit by bit, the drone dissolves, too. My heart thumps and my cheeks ache from clenching my teeth.

I run my hands over the ground around my body.

There are no autumn leaves, just dry, thirsty grass. The pine tree above is the only one around, the one I'd hugged minutes ago. I am in a garden, not the woods. I look back up into the sky, searching for something else to focus on, to keep the memory from coming back. But the sparkle of a few stars is the only possible distraction. His image, his smell, his voice will not go away, even though I know he's not here.

Shhh!

I sit up, put my head in my hands, and cry. "Just go away!"

I cry till I no longer have energy for even a sniffle. When I reach into my back pocket for a tissue, I feel the warm glow of *Resurrecting the Dragon*. I pull it out, put my hand on the cover, and close my eyes again.

"Like it or not, I'm just like Sarah. We're members of the same Unfortunate Club." The memory was never forgotten. It's always simmered just below the surface, and I worked really hard keeping it down there so it wouldn't overflow into my consciousness and become real, make a mess. It spoke in a loud voice that I refused to listen to. Until now.

"You are not broken," Sister G had told her little sister. Sarah was a survivor, just like Kalice in *Resurrecting the Dragon*. So, I must be a survivor, too.

But did I have enough fire in me, like Kalice did, to do battle with him, to even face up to him?

I open my eyes. The silhouettes of sunflowers stand tall along the fence on the other side of the garden. Sister G told me that fear never really goes totally away, but every girl has the power within her to live with it and all the other emotions she may have. It takes bravery and trust. I think I can trust a flower though I'm not sure about the bravery thing yet.

I choose the sunflower on the far left. It stands a few inches taller than me, but I'm able to reach up and touch its center. The black spiky seeds tingle, but I hold my fingers there anyway and close my eyes.

"Spirit, help me embrace my superpower. I know it's inside of me. I just can't quite grab it." I breathe in all the scents of the garden—roses, herbs, and yes, even the pine—allowing them to infuse my body with their energy. Trust it to work its magic, I tell myself, even though that pine scent keeps trying to override the herbs and roses.

Breathe in for four counts, hold for seven, exhale for eight. In through the nose, out through the mouth. I repeat Mimi's breathwork, and soon my body feels full, yet light, and I open my eyes. The sunflower droops a bit. I thank it for sharing its spirit.

I turn around and face the pine tree again, then take a few baby steps toward it, to a place like where it happened, years ago, in the woods, behind a different building.

"I'm safe," I tell myself. "I'm nowhere near that place."

But my body acts like I *am* there. It wants to turn and run away, but my legs are like cement blocks. So, I freeze and focus on my feet so I won't see that tree.

And there is the dragonfly, perched on my sandal, looking at me with his enormous eyes. They've lost their creep-factor and don't look like an extraterrestrial's now. Now they look wise. The dragonfly flutters his wings, urging me to keep on going.

I pick up one foot at a time, the dragonfly still with me, each step dropping like a stone till I get to the pine tree. A voice mumbles something mean, and I stop right there.

Shhh!

I cover my ears and whisper, "I can't do this. I just want him to go away."

Grey Cat snakes around my legs and purrs. Then everything goes still, as if waiting for me to do what I need to do.

Slowly, I reach out my shaky arm and point. Is he there behind the tree?

I step back too fast and trip, but catch myself before going down. I move further and further away from that tree.

Grey Cat's still purring. The dragonfly flits from my foot to my shoulder, and the sunflowers lean toward me, watching my every move. I feel the garden urging me on with its mighty breath, but my body resents the push. It remembers, even if my mind doesn't want to.

With a shudder, I move forward again until I'm face-to-face with the tree. I open my eyes super wide even though I know seeing him will hurt. Then, bit by bit, I let the image take shape.

His black sneakers with red laces. His torn jeans, dirt caked on the knees. His hoodie with the Stonewall Tennis Team logo on the front. The scratchy stubble on his chin. Dark eyes that have no bottom. Breath stinking of cigarettes. Cousin Jimmy.

I point at him. He sneers.

I hide my face with my forearm. "I can't do this."

But behind my arm, I see another image. Me and Sister G. We're sitting in this garden, on the bench. Sister G is handing me her book.

I uncover my eyes. He is still here. I despise him, how smug he is, and how small and confused I feel.

I stab my index finger at him. He laughs.

I back off again, squeezing my palms shut. Then I open them and stare at my hands, indentations where my nails had dug in. The longer I stare, the rosier my palms get until finally, streams of fire snake from my fingers like mini lightning bolts. I aim my hands at Jimmy, spin the fire round and round him, wrapping him in tendrils of heat, forward and backward, over and over again. He grimaces and writhes until he finally dissolves into the ground, a silent pile of ash at my feet.

"I'm safe now," I whisper.

The sunflowers sing out, "Louder! Louder!"

I square my shoulders and put my hands on my hips.

"Swiha!" I call out, just short of a shout since the nuns are asleep.

The pine tree shudders. Grey Cat settles onto my feet. His purr tickles my toes.

I am in charge now, and I need to show it.

"Swiha!" I scream, pointing at the pile of ashes under the pine tree. "You warned me not to tell, and that's exactly what I'm going to do. I will never allow secrets to steal my spirit again."

The ashes rise, swirl around, and drift away. I drop my arm and heave a sigh.

The moon makes shadows across the garden and every so often a daisy or rose bush ducks under them as if settling under a blanket before sleep. My body is drained, like after doing the mile run in PE. The fatigue is intense but satisfying.

I finished what I needed to do—without a plan! But there is still more to be done. I wipe my runny nose on my sleeve and head toward the gate on wobbly legs.

"See you tomorrow, Grey Cat."

The garden gently exhales me through the gate, a carpet of pink petals under my feet. Petals. They have to be shed before new roses can bloom. Just like shedding a secret so a new life can begin. I close the gate, inhale deep, and walk home through the quiet night.

CHAPTER NINETEEN

When I wake in the morning, I look around my room. Something is different. It isn't Felix. He's chomping on hay in his cage, as usual. All three of Mimi's matryoshka dolls are peeking out at me from their proper place on their bookshelf. I get out of bed and go to the bathroom to brush my teeth. In the mirror, I look the same. One unbelievable night in Sister G's garden wouldn't change that. My hands tremble as I squeeze the toothpaste onto the brush, but that's to be expected after what I'd gone through. I hold up my toothbrush, open my mouth, and that's when I realize it.

Silence!

There's no more noise in my head. No more voices. No more bad stuff bubbling away deep down inside of me. I am all cleared out. Now I just need to get back to the garden to follow up on my plan for Sister G.

I tell my mother that I'm going to the convent to see if there's any news about Sister G. She seems fine with it. Maybe I shouldn't have assumed she wouldn't be. I promise myself that I'll tell her all about everything later. It feels good to let go of secrets. Lighter. Warmer.

My instincts prove correct. When I track down Grey Cat, there's a new note wrapped around his collar. I untie it and offer him some catnip. He nibbles it and rolls around in the garden while I read the note.

Sister G wants me to meet her at eleven a.m. by the basement door inside the library. I didn't even know there was a door in the basement. She's drawn a map showing it hidden between two of the temporary bookshelves holding the young adult graphic novels. The town wants blood, and I hope Sister will be safe coming back here.

I go straight to the basement and look around the stacks, but don't see a soul. Setting off on a search, I walk all around the perimeter, peeking around shelves as I go, looking for the graphic novels.

I stop cold.

Just around the corner in front of me is Adeline, sitting on the floor, tucked behind the front page of a newspaper. No sign of her kitten. A twinge of sadness makes my legs weak. Doesn't Adeline belong anywhere? Why is she always here at the library? I turn to go back the way I'd come.

"Pssst!"

I peek back over my shoulder. It isn't Adeline.

It's Sister G!

A pair of dark glasses sit on top of her head—she has hair! And regular clothes. No habit. She waves me over. As soon as I sit down next to her, I lose it.

"Sister G, I am so sorry," I gush. "I never should have—"

"Hush," Sister whispers. "Everything is fine." She folds up the newspaper, stands, and looks all around. She pulls her sunglasses over her eyes, then waves at me to follow her. On the far side of the basement, she pushes aside a nearly empty rack of books, exposing a door. She reaches above the door and fumbles around, coming away with a key that opens the lock. We enter the room. A waft of musty air pushes me back. I rub my eyes, and when they clear, I see stacks and stacks of books.

"The home for rare and elderly books," Sister G explains. "This room is fireproofed with nice, thick walls. We can talk in private here."

We settle ourselves into a corner. "Please," I beg, "tell me how to make things right between us again."

Sister G shakes her head. "Things are right just as they are. The convent wasn't so much an aspiration as it was a hideout for me. Thanks to you, I realize that now."

I squirm, not sure I deserve any thanks at all.

"I thought I could escape all my difficult feelings by retreating," Sister says. "It didn't work."

"But now what will you do? Where will you go?"

"Not sure yet."

I'm finally here with Sister G, just as I'd hoped, and I can't figure out how to tell her what happened last night in her garden. I look around at all the books that have been saved from the fate of decay and old age or even theft. Where are the brave words I need to speak?

Then I spot something else.

"Whoa!" I shout as I jump to my feet.

There, neatly stacked in a corner behind, but not hidden by some thick gold-edged books, is a stack of about fifteen *Resurrecting the Dragon* books.

"Your books!" I exclaim.

Sister G's hand flies to her mouth and she shakes her head in amazement.

Just then, the door slowly slides open, and we freeze. Caught like rats in a trap.

But it's only Adeline. She raises her brows, and her eyes are round as quarters. She turns around quickly to leave.

Sister G stops her. "Adeline, you're welcome to stay. Just close the door behind you."

We watch as she pulls a copy of *Resurrecting the Dragon* from her bag and places it neatly on top of the others.

I spin around to Sister G. "She did it! She's the censor!" I turn to Adeline. "But why? Why did you steal the books?" I don't know whether to be happy to have found the censor or sad to know it was this woman I'd always considered a target of injustice.

Adeline faces us and holds up her hands in the classic "stop" pose. She shakes her head and points at the books.

"No what?" I ask her. "Don't deny that you took the books. How else would you know where they were all hidden?"

Adeline mouths some silent words and makes a lot of hand movements, exposing a tattoo of a dove on one of her wrists. The more Adeline gestures, the more her eyes jump between Sister G and me, not sure where to land. My eyes flare at the fact that she'd robbed Sister G and Sarah's stories from them, and I hope Adeline could feel the burn.

Sister G pulls her journal from her back pocket, turns to a blank page, and hands it and a pencil to Adeline. "Write what you'd like to say."

Why is Sister G being so patient with her? My breath comes in short bits as we wait for Adeline to finish. Whatever excuse she has won't be good enough for me.

Finally, Adeline hands the journal back to Sister G, who reads it aloud.

"I am not a thief. I am a rescuer. My daughter, Jill, read *Resurrecting the Dragon* and loved it. She loved it so much that she wrote her own story on the blank pages in the back of the book and returned it to the library. Every week she'd check to see if another girl had added a story, and she ultimately read about three others who'd also been abused. Then one week when she came to check the book, all the pages on which the girls had written their stories had been torn out. Someone defaced some of the original pages so badly that you couldn't read the words or understand what the pictures were saying. That's when I decided that I would protect the girls' voices and the stories they told, many of them for the very first time. So, I biked to as many libraries as I could, took the books, and hid them here in this room. I'm in the library enough, so I knew nobody used this room anymore. And I easily found the key on the hook above the door frame. I guess you figured that out, too."

I grab the journal from Sister G and shake it at Adeline. "But when you supposedly saved the stories by taking them from the shelves and hiding them, you also kept them from others who might've wanted to read them." Adeline just looks at the ground and I think I hear her sniffle.

"Plus," I say, "you ended up smothering your daughter's chance to tell her story again in one of the other books. How could you do that?"

Adeline snatches the journal from me and writes as if her life depends on it. She hands it back, and I read it aloud.

"I couldn't bear to see people stealing Jill's and other girls' stories. I planned to collect enough copies and tape more blank pages into them, then put them back on the shelves where, hopefully, more girls would discover them and then safely speak up."

Adeline nudges her bag with her foot. This woman, whom I thought of as shy and scared, has a strong will. Maybe that's the way a mother behaves when somebody messes with her daughter. Sometimes people do something wrong for the right reason.

I continue reading Adeline's words. "I hoped someone like you would come along and be pushy enough to want to find the book. Because I knew when that happened, the unspoken subject of abuse would have a good chance of becoming part of a conversation that might help end it."

Just like Emerson said. *Every burned book enlightens the world.*

"I'm sorry for accusing you of doing something wrong, Adeline," I told her. "What you did is something amazing and I thank you so, so much." Sister G nods.

Adeline hugs me, waves at Sister G, and leaves. I think about Adeline's words as I gaze at the stack of *Resurrecting the Dragon* books. Adeline had a plan and was determined to carry it out. I realize plans don't always turn out right, and plenty of times you have to think on your feet to change the plan to get back on track. That's what Adeline had to do. Same with me and Sister G.

I sit down next to the stack of books, take one from the middle, and open it. Sister G sits next to me. We read the back pages of every single copy of

Resurrecting the Dragon, every one whose pages are still intact, that is. Then I look up at Sister G.

"Now what do we do?"

Sister G hugs her knees and thinks for a while.

"You look so different in pants and a shirt, and you have hair!" I say, to break up the seriousness. "You're like a new person."

Sister smiles and finally speaks. "A new person with a fresh start ahead. I know what I have to do. First, I need to say a proper goodbye to my friends at the convent. I won't apologize for writing *Resurrecting the Dragon*, but I will ask for their forgiveness for turning their world upside down and causing them so much suffering."

Sister G is definitely embracing her Fear Part.

"Then I suppose I must carry on, perhaps along the same lines as Adeline's plan. I'll publish more books, get them back on the shelves. Pray that girls will continue to read and respond."

"Still, anybody can steal them just like they always have. How do you stop censorship? Seems impossible."

"We just continue to do the smalls things we're able to do. They'll add up."

That stack of books seems to be staring at me. The copy in my lap tingles. There is something I need to do right this very second.

I open the book to the blank pages at the end. I look up at my friend, who smiles and hands me her pen with *RTD* engraved on it.

• • •

Sister G sits with me until I finish writing. Then I clear my throat and read my story to her. Out loud. The entire thing.

I shudder and cry non-stop. I couldn't control it if I tried. And I don't try. When my exhausted body settles down, Sister holds my face in her hands and says, "You are so strong. Perfect, just as you are."

I cry until there are no more tears left. Sister G has a faraway look in her eyes, and she's fingering her beads.

"So, Jett, even though you've allowed that piece of your life to be remembered, and you've felt all the feelings it brought up, the sound of a plane and the smell of pine needles and autumn leaves may still scare you. But in time, the fear will float to the back, and you'll be in charge again. Meanwhile, you are now officially a part of the community of Brave Girls. Your spirit is not broken. Your soul is intact. Maybe there's something you want to do with that knowledge."

I shrug. My mind is all cloudy, but I know in time I'll sort things out. I rub the book cover with my thumb. "Well, for one thing, I've got to talk to my parents about all this. Mimi would want me to because she always said stories need to be shared."

"Your parents will want to know. They'll want to help you." She holds the blue bead separate from the others and nods. "Yes, let them help."

"They won't like hearing it, but it's the only way I can start fresh."

"Fresh starts are full of possibilities. Like one season melting into the next."

I place the book on the top of the stack, line it up just right with the others. "They've been through a lot, these books, just like we have... which gives me an idea." Sister G tips her head, her eyes curious. "What if you give the *book* a fresh start? Why not change the book's title? Call it *Beads on a Necklace*, seeing as it started as Sarah's story, and others are adding to the chain."

Sister G smiles, a crinkly sort of one, happy in a weary way, but a little bit sad too.

"*Beads on a Necklace*. It's perfect. Thank you, Jett."

But really, it's all thanks to Sister G. And to the girls before me who were brave enough to tell their truths. My story is now where it belongs. Outside of myself, still a part of me, but narrated in my own voice.

Baby matryoshka, free at last.

CHAPTER TWENTY

The community garden buzzes with birds, butterflies, and the excited voices of us girls.

"Okay, my young tour guides," Sister G calls. "Let's get ready to welcome our first visitors."

"Be sure to show them the graffiti wall," Dava, the social worker, adds. "We want anyone who feels so moved to add to it."

For the past few weeks, Sister G and Dava have been leading our Brave Girls Book and Garden Club. We have about a dozen members. Local therapists and doctors referred some, and others are just friends who care. *Beads on a Necklace* is only one book we'll read, and there'll be plenty more. Our discussions always take place here as long as the weather's good. Afterwards, we work and hang out in the garden.

"Jett! Come help me straighten this sign," Thellie yells, pointing to the explanation about how our graffiti wall came to be. So far, there are only a few things painted on the giant brick wall behind the abandoned factory. But I know it'll transform just as pretty as this garden has.

Rodney's passing out copies of the map he sketched, giving visitors a bird's-eye view of the community garden with all the plantings labeled. I see my family and wave to them. Bo and Jack are unusually still, actually standing in one place. When I talked to my parents about Cousin Jimmy, they included my brothers in the conversation. I'm sure it was hard for everyone to hear my story, but Mom said our family needs to communicate better, and it needed to start right then. They all knew Jimmy was a bully, and that he'd done some mean things to animals, but nobody, including my parents, thought he'd go so far as to hurt me like he did. I realize now more than ever that silence is not always peaceful and not always right.

"Welcome to the Wisteria Community Garden!" Sister G announces. "This special day highlights the opening of a sanctuary where all can congregate, discuss, and of course plant, tend, and flourish."

Sister points to the factory. "You might think that the backyard of an old factory is a funny place for a community garden, but we believe it's the perfect spot! During WWII, many in our town were employed here making parachutes. And like parachutes, gardens have the ability to slow a body down when we're moving too fast, providing a safe way to land on our feet during troubled times." She breathes in deeply through her nose. "So with that, I now turn you over to your trusted tour guides for the day. Girls?" She motions us over and we each guide a group of people along the gravel paths that wind all around the yard.

I lead my family, pointing out and naming the flowers and vegetables we've planted. Finally, we reach the far end, the quietest spot in the community garden, where the graffiti wall is.

"Which bricks did you paint, Jett?" Bo asks.

I point to the top left corner of the wall, the highest I could reach without a stool. On a series of bright green bricks are these words that I painted in blue: Even in the mud and scum of things, something always, always sings. RWE

"A Ralph Waldo Emerson quote," my dad says. "Beautiful choice."

"Hopeful," Mom adds.

I nod. "Yeah. This wall didn't fit in with the garden because it's just so... so not-alive. We decided to transform the bricks into a wall that speaks, or I guess Emerson would say, it sings. A graffiti wall where anyone can speak and be heard."

Jack and Bo catch a glimpse of a monarch butterfly and follow it around the garden. Slowly. On tiptoe. I look way up past the wall, beyond the tops of the oak trees, and close my eyes. *Mimi, have the twins transformed somehow? Or is it just me? Even with this crowd of people wandering around, chatting, and looking at flowers, this place feels like peace to me.*

I guess I'll always wonder about what's behind the mystery of how and why everything changes. Maybe there is no answer, and maybe I can learn to be okay with that. But there is one thing that I am absolutely, positively sure of. Ralph Waldo Emerson *is* alive. He lives on inside every one of us who trusts their feelings enough to speak their true story.

Think about it. It's no secret.

THE END

(Of my story. Feel free to tell yours below.)

Beads on a Necklace by
(Your name here)

AUTHOR'S NOTES

Like matryoshka dolls, there is a story nested within Jett's story, a personal truth that's alive within the fiction. Like Jett, I am a survivor of childhood sexual abuse. I wrote *Jett Jamison and the Secret Storm* long after I wrote many other very raw pieces that helped me process my trauma. You see, not only had my abuser demanded that I not tell, but when I finally sought help as an adult, I was unable to speak about what happened to me. My wise therapist, Judith, encouraged me to write, and it's thanks to her that now, ten years later, I'm writing books for kids.

When I was a child, I never came across any children's books that addressed trauma. If I had, I might have spoken up and gotten help much earlier. I might've known that sexual abuse is not uncommon, and that a victim should feel no shame. Perhaps reading about other girls like me would've given me the strength to share my story and ease the burden of the secret I carried for many years. At the very least, I wouldn't have felt so alone.

I hope children connect with Jett's story, whether they've been abused or know someone who has been, and that they understand there is hope for healing, and there are resources for help. Perhaps Jett will serve as a teacher to all, opening up a conversation that is long overdue, reminding us not to make assumptions about the way a person behaves when we don't yet know their story.

Remember, when you choose to add your story to the other beads on the necklace, you become a part of the community of brave girl voices. This means you're never really alone anymore. I'm so grateful to all the survivors who've shared their stories with me. They remind me of the power inherent in every voice, and the necessary message our joined voices can convey.

If you've been abused, please tell a trusted adult. There are many organizations out there who can help, like these:

24/7 confidential hotline: 1-800-656-HOPE (4673)
Website: Online.rainn.org

State by state resources:
https://www.nsvrc.org/find-help

And speaking of help, no book of mine was, or ever will be, written solo. I'm so grateful to family and friends who have supported me and my writing. If it weren't for them, this book wouldn't exist.

Thanks to the Black Rose team for believing in this book and working hard to get it into children's hands.

Elizabeth Strazar, you helped me understand and welcome all aspects of my story and creatively transform those ragged-edged pieces into a cohesive whole. Thanks to your calm and ever-present encouragement, Jett absorbed it all and was able to tell her own story in detail, with love.

Over the past few years, I've spent many, many hours at the Blackstone Library, where most of this book was written. The building itself is magical and was an inspiration for Jett's story. I give thanks to the staff and librarians for supporting my work and the work of all authors, and especially for providing children with a safe, non-judgmental space where they can explore, ask questions, and have fun.

Over nearly five years, Jett's story changed shape with the support of teachers, critique partners, and beta readers whose insights were invaluable. Leah Andelsmith, once again your part in birthing a Brave Girl was invaluable. Ona Gritz, Dee Hahn, Mare Hagarty, Caitlin Jans, Janet Morrison, Linda Davis and Jamie Potter, you gave me many hours of your time, reading and offering feedback on how to bring forth Jett's voice and story in the most authentic and engaging way.

Gretchen Street, your voice was always there in the back of my mind, cheering me on, reminding me what strength and bravery really means.

My Regal House/Fitzroy family has been an incredible source of positivity, infusing me with the strength to go forward with this book. Thank you all for being such kind literary friends.

Nicholas and Gregory, I thank you for your empathy, love, humor, and never-ending support of me. Chip, you've stood by my side for over forty years; you've been my rock during rough times and never wavered. Having you three guys close by always warms my heart and soothes my soul.

P.S. Though he is no longer with me, I would be remiss if I didn't send gratitude to my pet rabbit Felix. He never uncovered Ralph Waldo Emerson quotes for me, but he was a wise and loving comfort.

Jett Jamison and the Secret Storm is the second book in Kimberly's *Brave Girl* collection. Part of the proceeds from this book will benefit the Blackstone Library in Branford, CT.

Connect with Kimberly on her website
kimberlybehrekenna.com

About the Author

After working as a detective's assistant, a breakfast cook (poached eggs are still her nemesis), a tae-kwon-do instructor, and an adolescent and family counselor, Kimberly taught fifth grade, her favorite job ever. Born, raised, and still residing on the Connecticut shoreline, she now writes children's books full time, always inspired by the power of play, thoughtful questions, and a life-long belief in nature's ability to heal. *Jett Jamison and the Secret Storm* is the second book in her *Brave Girls Collection*. Connect with her at kimberlybehrekenna.com

Note from Kimberly Behre Kenna

Word-of-mouth is crucial for any author to succeed. If you enjoyed *Jett Jamison and the Secret Storm*, please leave a review online—anywhere you are able. Even if it's just a sentence or two. It would make all the difference and would be very much appreciated.

Thanks!
Kimberly Behre Kenna

We hope you enjoyed reading this title from:

CPSIA information can be obtained
at www.ICGtesting.com
Printed in the USA
BVHW042013210723
667625BV00001B/13